T0288626

IN COMMAND

BOOK THREE

AN AUNARE CHRONICLES NOVELLA

USA *TODAY* BESTSELLING AUTHOR

AILEEN ERIN

INK MONSTER 🐼 AUSTIN, TX

INK MONSTER

First Published by Ink Monster LLC in 2021

Ink Monster LLC
100 Commons Rd., Ste 7-303
Dripping Springs, TX 78620
www.inkmonster.net

ISBN 9781943858613

Copyright © 2021 by Ink Monster LLC

All rights reserved. This book or any portion thereof
may not be reproduced or used in any manner whatsoever
without the express written permission of the publisher
except for the use of brief quotations in a book review.

CHAPTER ONE

AMIHANNA

A BEEPING WOKE ME, but it wasn't enough to pull me fully from sleep. I rolled over, curling deeper into the sheets.

But then came footsteps. I slowly stopped my movements under the covers. I didn't want to alert whoever had come into my room, but I was aware that I might be in for a fight.

I held my breath, waiting as the footsteps came closer.

Waiting for the right moment.

Waiting for them to get a little closer.

Wait—

Someone shook my shoulder.

Now.

I threw myself from the bed, hit a warm body, and quickly pinned it to the ground. Whoever was in my room thought they could catch me when I was asleep, but I never slept. Not deeply. Not when the threat of assassination was high.

I pressed my forearm across a neck and tried to see in the dark.

Damn it. What was the Aunare word for lights again?

Hands pushed at my arm, but I held it firmly in place. Whoever this was, they weren't getting away.

"Shit, babe." The voice was strangled—for obvious reasons—and strained, but familiar. Really familiar. "Wake up."

Wait. I was an idiot. Lorne had switched his room comp to Earther English. "Lights, twenty percent."

The lights eased on, stopping just above dim. The room came into view.

This used to be Lorne's suite, but now it was ours. The lamp beside the bed gave off enough light to hurt my eyes for a second, and then I glanced at who I had pinned.

"Shit." I immediately moved my arm and rolled away. "What the hell, Roan? Why are you sneaking into my room?"

"You can't *what the hell* me. That's my line. What the hell was that?" He rubbed his neck. "I think I might get a bruise right here. Is it red? Can you see?"

He always said that, but Roan was incredibly hard to bruise. "No. It's not red."

I was finally fully awake and realized my heart was racing. I rubbed my eyes, and I took a breath, trying to slow my heart a little. Everything was fine. I was fine. But I'd nearly killed my best friend.

"Sorry. I didn't know it was you."

He shot me a look that told me he was only moderately pissed off, which was good. "Who else would it be?"

"SpaceTech spies? Jason Murtagh finally coming to finish the job? Or—I don't know—another guard that decided I was better dead than as their future queen? The list of people who want me to stop breathing is pretty long, my friend."

Roan laughed at me like assassins hadn't tried to kill me just a few days ago. Some of them my own guards. Ditto on the SpaceTech spies.

"You must've really been sleeping hard because none of those people you just listed would've bothered to ring your doorbell."

Oh. Right. Fair point.

"I didn't hear it." Except I remembered the beeping. It had been woven in with my dreams and hadn't fully registered as my doorbell, but I couldn't say I didn't hear it. "And even if I did hear a doorbell, ignoring it means *go away*. I was *sleeping*."

Roan sat up and grabbed his tablet from where he'd dropped it. Or maybe I'd knocked it from his hands. Whatever. I glanced at it, and the screen seemed fine, as did Roan. Thankfully. I wasn't sure what I would do if I'd hurt him.

Other than throwing him into a healing pod and apologizing profusely.

"You don't have time for sleeping in today." He stood and reached a hand down. "It's my first official day as your assistant, and I'm going to do my job."

I groaned, instantly regretting giving him said job. I thought we could mostly spend time hanging or training, but if he woke me up, then I guessed there was more to my life now.

I took in my best friend. He was wearing a button-down shirt and some nice pants. His active shoes were replaced with something nicer. Was that leather? His hair was in tiny, tight curls, instead of its usual poofy mess.

He grinned at me, his white teeth standing out against his darker skin. "I look nice, right?"

"Man, your ego isn't hurting at all is it?" But that's exactly what I'd been thinking.

He looked really nice. The only jobs he'd had on Earth required clothes that he could get dirty in. I guessed I hadn't really thought about what he'd wear to this job, but clearly, he'd thought about it a lot. He looked like a whole new Roan.

I took his hand, and he pulled me to my feet. Now that the threat was gone, I wanted to crawl back into bed but somehow restrained myself.

Mostly because Roan put himself between me and the bed. "No, you can't get back in there. I just got you out, and you have an hour to get dressed and eat. I figured it used to take you ten to do both on Earth, but you gotta get pretty. I mean, I don't know if you can reach the level of my pretty today, but you should definitely give it a shot. And then we have to be out of here."

I ignored the fact that my best friend thought he was prettier than me and moved on to what he was really getting at. I rubbed my temples, trying to make myself think. I needed to be dressed up and out of here for something? But I couldn't remember anything. Whatever it was, it sounded like something I did *not* want to do. Anything that wasn't training wasn't my bag.

I'd only been awake for minutes, and already I could tell this day was going to be a pain. I had to ask a question, and I didn't want the answer to it.

"Why?" I held my breath, hoping he'd tell me quick, like ripping-off-a-bandage quick.

"High Council meeting." Roan could read me like no other. The words were out fast as if that would make them sting less. "They said they needed a four-hour block of your day."

Oh man. I really, really wished he hadn't woken me up. I could've slept for another few hours and missed it.

Wait.

"A four-hour block? *Four hours*? Are you serious right now?" What could possibly take four hours?

"Well, you did say we needed to declare war on SpaceTech. So, best guess, they want to talk to you about that, but there's no official set agenda. At least none that they shared with me."

I did want to declare war on SpaceTech, but if they wanted four hours, that meant they were going to fight me on it.

Kill me now.

"Where's Lorne?" Because I wasn't going anywhere without him.

"Hang on." He glanced down at his tablet. "Fynea sent me a link to his cal so we could coordinate schedules if needed. Checking…" He tapped a few times. "Okay. This says he had a call starting two hours ago."

"Two hours ago?" I shoved past Roan and sat on the bed.

"Come on, Am. We don't have time for this."

I wanted to be good and listen to him, but the white sheets were soft and silky and begging for me to crawl back inside their cocoon of sleep. I tried to resist—I really did—but it felt early. Painfully early.

I tugged the covers over my legs, but Roan yanked them down.

"Just one more hour." My voice was a smidge whiny, but I couldn't help it.

"No. You don't have time for that. I already let you sleep in," Roan said.

My eyes started to grow heavy. Maybe I was still recovering from the last few days, but I didn't think that was it. I didn't even remember Lorne leaving this morning, and that stung a little. I wished he'd woken me up so that I'd know he wasn't here. Instead, I was left missing him and feeling a little empty.

I grabbed his pillow and snuggled deep.

Ugh. I was pathetic. I just needed more sleep. "What time is it?"

"The second sun just rose." Roan's tone was getting more frustrated, but I was right. It was brutally early, and yet I was a slacker for not being awake already?

Or maybe Lorne was just an overachiever? I guessed I'd find out soon enough. It'd only been days since I moved into Lorne's suite. Not nearly long enough to get into a rhythm.

I painfully dragged myself out of bed again and went to the curtains, pushing them open.

Two suns lit the morning sky, giving everything a slightly rosy hue. Lorne had an awesome view of the gardens and the fountain of me. I wondered if he'd put the statue there so he could see it, but that would be a little stalkerish. Or maybe it was sweet? I didn't know. I was thinking about wandering through the estate to find him so that I could get a proper good morning, so maybe I was just as bad.

I moved through the bedroom and into the living room beyond it. There was a massive u-shaped couch facing a large mid-screen. There was a fireplace off to one side and a round table with four chairs on the other. But none of that was what I needed.

I walked to the small fridge and grabbed a chilled bottle of *wyso*. It was the closest thing that the Aunare had to coffee, but it was much, much stronger. I learned the hard way that if I drank too much too early, I'd be wired and forget to eat.

After a few sips, I felt much more human. "What's the High Council meeting going to be like?"

"I'm not sure exactly." Roan leaned against the back of the couch, typing on his tablet. He paused to look up at me. "It'll be my first meeting, too. We both read through the digital packet on the council members and details on it, but honestly, it didn't feel like it gave me enough intel on what it'd be like to actually go to a meeting. Want me to message Fynea and ask for some tips?"

The stubborn side of me screamed to refuse the help. I could do this on my own. I knew I could. But that was me being stubborn. Knowing when to ask for help was a sign of strength.

"Yes, please." I started toward the bathroom. "I'm going to shower."

"Good. I'll wait here and order you some food, too."

I paused, turning back to him for a second. "I can't go to the kitchens?" I always went by the kitchens in the morning to grab something from the market-size pantry.

Roan winced, and I knew I wasn't going to like what he said next. "So, um, last night, Plarsha talked to me. I guess the kitchen staff sort of feels uncomfortable with you in there now that you're going to be the High Queen."

"What?" They didn't feel comfortable? Plarsha had been my nanny before I'd been stuck on Earth, but now she managed the entire estate. If she said the kitchen staff were uncomfortable with me in the kitchens, then I knew they were. But why? "Did I do something to piss them off?"

"I don't think it's like that. She didn't seem upset, but the Aunare are more formal than we are. Plarsha said we needed to let the staff take care of you now, and when you show up in the kitchens, it's like saying they're sucking at their job. That you don't trust them to bring you food that you'd enjoy."

My mouth dropped open. "What?" That was some insane logic. "I just don't like bothering anyone. It's so much easier if I just go to the kitchen and grab what I want to eat. I don't need anyone to wait on me. They're too busy to—"

"Their main job is to feed you, your parents, and Lorne. That's it. And you're not letting them do their primary job."

"But they're not just feeding the three of us. They have to provide meals for all the other million people that live on the estate or visit it during the day."

"Right. But they see it as a privilege to cook for you. Feeding you is the top of the top jobs for the Aunare. You're not letting them do their job, and the Aunare are all about doing their jobs. Because it's not a job, it's a vocation. A passion."

I guessed I could see his point, but I didn't like it. I knew things would change around the estate, but it was happening too fast. It'd only been three days since I'd put Lorne's ring on my finger, and already everything was different. Lorne wasn't here when I woke up. Instead, Roan was here telling me what all I had to do today, which was nothing fun. I wouldn't have minded it if I was doing four hours of training with my guards. But this High Council meeting was going to be awful. The digital packet had done nothing to make me believe it could be anything else.

And now I couldn't even get my own food?

I didn't like relying on someone else, even if that person's job was to be there for me. It felt weird. It was the exact opposite of what I was used to.

"I'm going to shower." I left the living room and didn't stop moving until I was inside the bathroom, letting the door slide closed after me, cutting off whatever Roan was saying.

I stripped off my nightclothes—a pair of shorts and a loose tank made out of the softest silky material—and stepped under the hot spray. This was the best part—one of the best parts of being on Sel'Ani. The showers. In my apartment on Earth, I'd used a quick wash cleaning spray. It did the job and wasn't as expensive as using water, but now I was getting spoiled.

As I washed my probably too-long hair, I tried to think of all the things here that I was grateful for. All of the things that made all the growing pains of becoming whoever I was supposed to be a little less painful.

Showers with clean, hot water. Obviously.

Lorne. He was top of the list. I never thought I could feel for anyone what I felt for him. I didn't have the words to properly describe the feeling, but it was more than love. The connection felt like it had a life of its own, and I was still trying to wrap my head around it.

I was safe here. Mostly. If I didn't think about assassins or SpaceTech spies or the war that threatened to wipe all the Aunare from existence, but at least I wasn't being overtly hunted here. That was something I wouldn't take for granted.

The food here was real, not like the synthetic Earther stuff. It actually made me feel full. Especially Nori's, Lorne's sister's cooking. It was like having the best of both worlds.

Maybe I could get her to send over a batch of enchiladas for dinner tonight. But would that upset the kitchen staff? Maybe I should give it a few days to smooth over whatever insults I'd unintentionally given them and then ask if I could have my favorite meal brought in?

Or I could ask them to make it, but what if they didn't know how?

Why did this have to be so complicated?

No, Amihanna. Back on track. I turned my face into the spray of water and thought of good things in my life again.

I was thankful for Eshrin, my head guard. He was so much fun to train with, and—funny enough—after the week I'd had, I kind of liked having guards. Except for traitor guards like Komae.

I remembered I needed to follow up with Eshrin on hiring new guards. Right now, Eshrin was the only one that I really trusted, but he couldn't work around the clock. And I couldn't have a team following me around all the time if I didn't trust them.

I added that to my mental to-do list—make sure Roan schedules time to get that together.

My wrist unit buzzed, and I swiped the water off my face to read it.

Roan sent a warning. I had ten minutes left.

Ice it all. "I'm hurrying," I yelled to him, not caring if he couldn't really hear me.

I cut the shower, wrapped myself in a towel from the warmer box, and walked into the adjoining closet.

It was massive, filled with rows of clothes. It curved around and had sections for different kinds of events. I should probably grab something more formal for the meeting, but being comfortable meant I would be more confident.

I reached for a pair of leggings.

"No! What are you doing?" a voice came from inside the closet.

I tightened my grip on the towel. "Who's here?"

A young, blonde woman with lightly browned skin came out from between two rows of dresses. "It's me. Almya."

Almya? The seamstress. I let out a breath.

Fine. Okay. I knew her, but what was she doing in my closet? "Did you need something?"

Her green eyes widened in surprise. "I don't need something, but you do. I'm here for you. I'm your official stylist starting today, remember? You have a meeting on your schedule with the High Council, and I'm here to make sure you're properly dressed."

"Right." But I didn't understand why she was here.

"As your stylist, I help you decide what to wear every day. That's my job now."

What? When did I say that would be the job? I liked picking out my own clothes. I mean, I didn't *like it*-like it, but it was much better than someone else telling me what to wear.

"I can't let you go to a meeting that important without the proper attire." She held out a dress. "Please. This is my dream job, and you can't kick me out on my first day." She shook the hanger at me.

Okay. I had a stylist now. Just one more thing to adjust to, but on a scale of okay to apocalypse, this was definitely not bad at all.

Except if she was going to insist that I wore dresses to everything. That wasn't going to happen.

I shook my head, stepping back from her. "Hard pass. If you're going to help me, I need you to understand that I don't wear dresses. Ever. I'm officially done with them."

The look on her face was so crestfallen and sad that it almost made me laugh.

I'd just have to explain, and then she'd understand. "I wore a dress every day for work on Earth, and I hated it. I made a promise to myself that I wouldn't wear another one if I ever got off that planet, and I can't, or I'd be breaking that promise. I don't feel comfortable in dresses, and if I'm not comfortable, then I won't come off as confident in the meeting. And that's—"

"—not acceptable."

"Exactly."

"Let me figure something else out for you."

"Are you almost dressed?" Roan shouted through the door. "You're going to be late, and you haven't eaten yet."

I dropped my chin to my chest and closed my eyes. Was this my life now?

Was this what I wanted?

Roan yelling at me about my schedule. Almya picking out my clothes. Lorne gone before I was even awake.

It was the last one that stung, but he had meetings. He had

stuff going on. He was the High King of the Aunare. It made sense that he had to get up early.

But as I stood there in my towel waiting for Almya to hand me my clothes for the day, I had reservations.

This didn't feel like me. This wasn't who I was.

And if it didn't feel like me, if this wasn't who I was, then what was I supposed to do next?

I wasn't sure, and that terrified me. I needed a second to figure out what I wanted, but as I stared at Almya and listened to Roan lecturing me to hurry up, I knew that I wasn't getting it today.

Not today, but soon. I was going to have to figure out what being the future High Queen was exactly and what I'd agreed to. I hoped I hadn't done anything I'd regret.

I could never regret being with Lorne, but the rest of it... The rest of it was a lot to digest, and it was only day one. Day one of my new forever.

Buckle up, Amihanna. Time to step up. If I could handle life on Earth post-Liberation Week, Abaddon, and overcoming my traumas, then I could do this.

Maybe.

Probably.

Ice it all.

CHAPTER TWO

LORNE

I WAS A MAN ENRAGED. I'd spent the last two days trying to hide it from Amihanna. She didn't need anything else to burden her, and yet, I kept hoping that she'd notice that I was inches from losing all grip on my control.

I wasn't sure I could take one more thing going wrong.

And yet, things kept going wrong.

After days of calls to allies who refused to join our fight against SpaceTech, I'd been counting on this call going well. I didn't think it was naïveté or blind hope, but I needed someone to see through SpaceTech's lies. Who better than the queen of a telepathic race? I knew if I could get her backing, the other allies would follow.

But the call had been a complete failure.

I hadn't gotten her approval. If anything, she seemed angry and insulted that I'd tried.

I paced in Rysden's living room now. His fireplace was lit, even though we reached daylight a few hours ago. Rysden always believed a fire would give comfort, and I needed any comfort I could get right now.

Except the heat of the fire seemed to fuel my anger.

My skin burned bright, and I knew if I didn't calm down, then I'd be in trouble. But I was already in trouble.

Rysden sat in one of the two massive armchairs facing the fire, watching me closely as I paced. His glass with ice clinked as he shook it. He looked calm and cool, but inside the glass was some fermented *tinka*. The table between the chairs held a large crystal decanter and another glass, but I wouldn't take it.

It was much too early to be drinking, and I knew my limits. If I started leaning on alcohol now, I would be on a dark path. It was hard, but I resisted the urge to sit in the other chair, pour a large serving into the waiting glass, and down it in one go.

"It was a nice effort, but it was a long shot to reach out to her," Rysden said from where he reclined in his chair. "Don't take this failure on yourself." He set his glass down on the table and motioned to the other seat.

I wasn't ready to sit. I still needed to pace. "I knew it was a long shot. Cheztkena is usually neutral, but she's broken away for great causes before. It seemed perfectly within her ability to break away again, especially now. No one can afford to stay neutral. Not anymore. Not when SpaceTech has so blatantly moved against us." I paused in front of him. "They attacked Ta'shena. They destroyed Sa'shotaem."

"I know."

I knew he knew, but he wasn't angry. Why was I the only one losing control? "They tried to steal Amihanna."

Rysden's skin started to glow.

There. Finally. Some actual proof that there was some anger beneath the surface.

"I'm very aware of how close to that goal they came." His words were sharply minced. "I'm very thankful that you saved her. Again."

I didn't want his thanks. I didn't need to be thanked, but we had to do something. This couldn't happen again.

"Our allies have become as complacent as my father. I thought that with Cheztkena's ability to read minds and see through all the politics that she might see that it was time for her people to take a stand. If she did, then everyone would follow." I wiped a hand down my face. "I'm an idiot for thinking it would be so easy. They're going to think I'm my father." And that was a true nightmare.

"Who will?" He sounded outraged at the idea, but it was fact.

Feeling more than a little defeated, I finally sank into the chair. "Everyone." The Aunare. SpaceTech. Our allies. Everyone was going to think that I was as worthless a leader as my father, and I wasn't sure how to make them see otherwise. "I haven't taken action yet, and it sends a message that this is okay. That SpaceTech's abuse and slaughter of our people will be tolerated. And it can't be. It won't be."

"Yes, but you have to act wisely." Rysden leaned toward me. "You need our allies to back you."

"Do I? Do I really need them?" I wasn't so sure that I did.

"You at least need them to say that they won't join SpaceTech when you break the alliance."

That stupid alliance. My father was the laziest, most cowardly person I'd ever met. Now that war was imminent, he predictably fled from his responsibilities, and for once, his cowardice benefited the Aunare. Now my father sat locked away in a vacation home, doing nothing but eating and drinking. It was supposed to be a punishment, but I knew his punishment actually suited him more than being king. At least the only harm he could do now was to himself.

I hoped he choked on whatever he was gorging on right now. I hoped he drank himself into a stupor and never woke up. Because he never should've been king.

Now, my hands were tied.

My father and Murtagh Sr. signed an alliance over thirty years ago when SpaceTech-Aunare relations first started budding. The problem was that Murtagh Sr. was able to get our allies to join this alliance. One of the bylaws said that if two parties in the alliance went to war, all of the allies would have to join the defensive side.

Because we didn't act immediately against the original aggressive stance against us thirteen years ago, precedence had been set. My father never officially declared a problem. Small skirmishes had flared over the years, but they were always overlooked because neither my father nor Murtagh Sr. acknowledged that they happened.

SpaceTech could—and according to Cheztkena, they would—argue that because of the precedence set by my father, our declaration of war would be deemed an act of aggression. Not defense.

I'd argued with her that the death and destruction of Sa'shotaem was much larger than any of the previous skirmishes and that the subsequent attack on Ta'shena was proof that Space-Tech was acting against us.

She brought up Liberation Week and then shut down every argument I had.

I'd been hoping that, at the very least, she would've understood why the timing had been too tight for me to declare war. I was appointed High King only hours after Sa'shotaem had been attacked, and that next day, I'd defended Ta'shena and then ended up in a healing pod. There was no time for me to declare war before the two-day declaration window was up.

But then she pointed out that the High Council was against war. She'd seen it on the news. If my own people didn't back the war, how was she supposed to?

The Aunare were working against me, and I wanted to scream and rage and fight, but none of that would do any good.

For now, I could only wait for SpaceTech to attack again. Then, by immediately declaring war, I'd hope our allies would accept that declaration as a defensive one, and then a united war against SpaceTech could begin.

But I was Lorne ni Taure. I was built to fight. To defend our people. To stand up against anyone that would do us harm. And here I was, handcuffed by some stupid alliance my idiot father drew up.

I had to wait?

I had to risk more people being injured or dying?

It was beyond infuriating.

"You have to calm down, Lorne." There was a warning in Rysden's tone, and the way he was watching me, I knew he was wondering if he was going to need to lock me up again.

His worry was misplaced. I'd never let myself lose control like I did thirteen years ago, especially now that Amihanna was here. "I'm under control."

"Are you? Can you say that honestly?"

Maybe not, but I was doing the absolute best that I could. "Is there anything in the laws that says I can abolish the alliance?" I asked, changing the subject to one infinitely more important. "Or maybe there's a way for the Aunare to exit the alliance?"

Rysden studied the fire for a moment as if he were mentally running through the entire accord. "There's nothing about abolishing it, and exiting would be seen as a hostile act."

That was exactly what I'd been trying to avoid. "There's always a way to end an alliance. It's always built in. We're just not seeing it. Maybe if we look at it from a different angle or take a different tactic or make a better argument... Maybe if I—"

"No." Rysden shook his head slowly, and for a fraction of a second, his facade slipped, and I could see the frustration brewing under his skin. "Your father and his team came up with this alliance so that he wouldn't have to wage war. There is no loophole. It was designed to protect him from any war, and if something did happen to force his hand, he wouldn't have to fight it. The allies would do that for him."

Every day I woke up thinking that I couldn't hate my father more, and then I learned something new and that hatred grew.

I didn't like that I had so much hate in my heart for any one person, but for him, I made an exception.

"Cheztkena said that the alliance holds true. That if and

when I declare war, if it's not motivated and an immediate reac-tion to SpaceTech's advances, then they will join SpaceTech." That was what had really gotten me upset, and Rysden had been forced to end the call before I lost all control, but maybe she'd been testing me and my response.

If so, had I passed? Or had I failed? Yet again.

"I was there both today and when the alliance was formed." Rysden's tone was very matter of fact. "I heard what she said, and she's right."

"Yes, but did you believe her? That even with all the evidence against SpaceTech that the alliance would side with them?" I desperately wanted to hang on to some shred of fading hope.

"Cheztkena has no reason to lie."

That last sliver of hope that one of our allies might stand with us disappeared.

"In fact, I'd go farther and say that she is incapable of lying." Rysden paused for a moment, and I let the truth of his words sink in.

I never thought that the Aunare would have to stand alone against SpaceTech, but now I knew better. It was a painful real-ization, and the regret that I didn't stand up to my father sooner was hard to bear. Add in the weight of this war and the responsi-bility for so many, and I wasn't sure I could do it. I wasn't sure what I should do.

How was I supposed to move forward from this? Should I wait to declare war, risking so many lives by doing so? Or should I act now and risk fighting not just SpaceTech, but our allies, too?

"I needed Cheztkena to back us. If I could just talk to her in person, then—"

"It won't do any good. I know you haven't dealt much with the people from the Naustalic system, but Cheztkena is the queen of a species that can read minds. I can't say for sure, but I'd wager that her abilities make it nearly impossible to lie. Her people simply don't tell lies. They're not naive, but they don't see the use in it because they're wasted words when they can so easily see through them. If she says that the beings of the Naustalic system will join forces with SpaceTech against us if you declare war today, then that's what will happen."

We could stand against SpaceTech. I was certain of that much —but the people of the Naustalic system were just as technologically advanced as we were. If we had to go against them, it would be an even match. Add in the sheer size of SpaceTech's force, and I wasn't sure we could win.

I was going to be sick. I'd been hoping Cheztkena had been testing me, but if she couldn't lie, then it wasn't a test. She and her people would stand against us if we acted now.

Which left me to wait for SpaceTech's next attack before I could declare war. That was unacceptable. "What about the attack on Sa'shotaem? Can we find a way to make it qualify even though the time limit has passed?"

"It's been a week."

I knew that. I *knew* it, but I couldn't accept that my father would be so stupid as to accept this timeline. Two days to declare war? For something so extreme, surely they gave more of an allowance.

There had to be an argument I could make. "I became king the next day. I had to speak to my people. I... I needed time." I took a breath. "All right. The attack on Ta'shena. That was three days ago. With that attack and Sa'shotaem so close together, don't you think that we could call together the alliance and make an argument that—"

"It's not what I think that matters," Rysden yelled the first bit before taking a breath. "The alliance was very specific. I warned your father against it, but he wouldn't *listen*." Rysden took another steady breath as if it were almost painful to get the words out. "It says very clearly that you must act within the time it takes for your home planet to pass two days. It's been three since Ta'shena's attack. The alliance gives no leeway in the timeline for the change of rulers. We are left to wait for one more attack, and now that you are High King, you must be ready to declare war immediately."

Of course, I'd be ready. The problem was that I didn't want to wait. "But—"

"This is my fault." Rysden took the glass again, drinking it down and slamming it back on the table. "It's my fault that I didn't prepare you. I didn't tell you about the timeline stipulation. Everything happened so fast, and I wasn't prepared for an attack on your coronation day in our capital. I was distracted by my daughter's attempted kidnapping and worried for her in the healing pod. I wasn't thinking of the clock that was ticking away and the time wasted. I should've acted in your stead while you were in the pod with her, and I failed you. As the Hand of the King, I failed you."

No. This wasn't his fault. "You've been by my side through all the bad times, and I cannot let you take this on yourself. It was my job to take a closer look at the alliance, and I hadn't read it through fully." I took a breath. "We were both unprepared, we both made mistakes, but we've learned from them. SpaceTech won't get lucky again."

Rysden turned, staring into the fire. "I have many regrets. I'm not sure I can ever make good on them to you or my daughter, but..." He took a breath and stood. "We will prepare, we will plan, and when the time comes, we will be ready."

I rose. "Have the fleet set to leave on a moment's notice."

"Yes. That I will do. But I can't launch fully unless SpaceTech starts to move into our territory."

"They can't say what we can do in our own territory. Get the ships out there at the borders. Do everything you can to prepare for war, up to the very line of breaking the alliance. I want every inch of space between our planets and theirs watched. The second they get close to us, I want you out there protecting our planets."

"Of course, your majesty." He bowed his head, fist to heart. "What are you going to tell my daughter? This inability to do something will eat at her. It is worse for her, I think. After everything to be unable to do something."

"I'm going to say nothing to her about any of this." I shook my head. "I'll tell her nothing of the alliance. She won't understand all the rules and laws."

"She'll understand them just fine." His tone was sharp with insult.

I held up a hand to keep back his anger. "My apologies." We both needed a moment to cool down. "That wasn't what I meant. Of course, she'd understand the laws. I didn't mean to speak on her intelligence. What I mean is that she won't agree with them. She won't understand why I'm letting them hamper me. She'd want to burn them all."

"Ah." He nodded. "She hates politics. It's not something that she had to deal with on Earth. She's very direct, and while I love that about her, she needs to be eased into this new role."

"And you think by taking her to a High Council meeting that you'll be easing her in?" The council was frustrating at best, and although it sounded like they held some power, the truth was that they didn't. Not really. Not now that I was king.

Rysden shrugged. "She's going to have to deal with them eventually. Better to start now. And she can scream at them without many consequences. If she screamed at our allies, the cost would be too high. The High Council will teach her some patience in her politics."

That plan might backfire on him.

Not telling her about the alliance and its rules might backfire on me.

And now I needed to work on fixing the Aunare's perception of the war so that the next time I talked to Cheztkena, I could tell her the Aunare backed the war fully.

But that wasn't true now. The Aunare weren't ready for war, and they weren't sure about their new almost-queen. My only hope was that her first interview would clear up all of that.

"When do we film the interview with Himani?" He was one

of the top reporters among us. He never went for the easy story
or gossip, but got to the heart of issues and helped many subjects
voice their stories. Beyond that, Himani interviewed Amihanna
when she was in the arena, and she trusted him. Above all else,
that had earned him the job of taking Amihanna's first formal
interview.

I wanted to make sure that Amihanna got to speak her story
and reach the Aunare before the war started. Our people needed
to see Amihanna as their leader, not as some interloper from
Earth. The media had been better about their reporting now that
they'd been freed of my father's ties, especially since her heroic
defense of Ta'shena, but there were still a few reporters
spreading lies about her. That needed to end. Now.

The Aunare needed to be united in this war, and right now,
they were anything but.

"The interview is set for three days from now, but I'm
working on getting it moved up."

Three days? It was supposed to happen yesterday. "What's
stalling it?"

"Fynea."

Right. That made sense. My best friend and head assistant
was fierce. She would personally approve every question
Himani asked, and negotiate the tone, length, approval process
for what was aired, and anything else she needed. She liked
having total control over my interviews, but gaining that took
time. "I'll talk to her. It's more important to get it done than
argue about having final say on every detail."

"Agreed, your majesty. As usual." He motioned to the door.
"Why don't you go see my daughter before the meeting? Get
centered again. You'll do no good for her or us in the meeting if
you show up as you are."

As I was? He meant out of control and ready to destroy
anyone who crossed me.

That was a fair point. Getting centered was probably a smart
idea.

I clicked on my wrist unit and found that she was still in our suite.

I headed to the door. "I'll see you in the meeting," I said without pausing to look back at him.

I needed Amihanna.

I talked to her about balance, but ever since I watched her fall from the roof of the ship, ever since I saw those men stealing my *shalshasa* in my capital city, I hadn't been able to catch my balance.

I wasn't sure I had the strength to keep my temper stable, and I was afraid of what Amihanna would think of me if she ever saw me at my worst.

So, I would hide that part of myself from her, just as I would hide the frustrations of this alliance from her until there was something we could do about it together.

As I walked, I breathed in measured breaths until the glow on my skin was all but gone.

For her, I would try to keep control.

For her, I would hide my pain.

For her, I could endure anything.

CHAPTER THREE

AMIHANNA

ROAN HAD ALREADY COME into the closet three times to tell me I was running late, but Almya and I were still arguing over clothes. I told her I'd rather go naked to the meeting than wear one of the "appropriate" dresses that she'd picked out for me to wear. She didn't seem to understand that I didn't care if there were pants under the skirt or pockets for weapons or pants that were so loose that they looked enough like a skirt to make it virtually a dress. Even if I could fight in the dress, it was still a *dress*.

Almya was getting emotional and insulted, and at first, I cared about her feelings, but now I didn't.

"Almya. I'm not wearing—"

A throat cleared, and I didn't even turn around. "Roan. Best friend or not, I'm going to murder you if you keep coming in here."

"Not Roan."

I glanced over my shoulder. Lorne.

He was leaning against the edge of the door, watching me with his aquamarine gaze that seemed to see through me. My heart picked up, and I could feel myself giving him a stupid grin, but I couldn't stop it. "Hey."

"Hi." His gaze ran down my body and slowly back up, heating every inch of me. "As fashion-forward as I usually am, I think it's probably best if you find something else for the meeting. Quickly."

I turned back to Almya, who was still smiling—although now it looked too forced—and holding out two dresses for me to choose from.

She held one out a little farther, giving it a little shake. "This one would look lovely on you, and it's perfect for the—"

I shook my head. "If you would just listen to me—"

"Amihanna. My love," Lorne said softly. "I've been standing here for a moment, and I heard more than enough about what's going on. The thing to remember—"

"Is that I hate dresses," I said to Almya, hoping that she would listen. "*Hate*. Dresses."

"That's not what I was going to say."

I turned to him, annoyed and struggling to remember that I wasn't annoyed at him. "What?"

"The thing to remember is that *you* are the future queen. Not Almya." He gave her a short, pitying glance before focusing on me again. "You decide what you do, what you say, what you wear." He slowly walked toward me as he spoke. "So, put something on already." He brushed a quick kiss on my lips.

It was nice. I wanted more. And—

Lorne tapped my nose. "Because the food is getting cold, and I think Roan might be having a panic attack about being late."

Roan? Shit. It was his first day, and I was going to make him—make *us*—look bad. I should—

Wait. Did he say food?

My stomach grumbled, but I was pretty sure only I could hear it. Especially since Almya was sputtering.

Lorne straightened and looked at Almya. "I know you're new and haven't had any training, but if you succeed at your job that means Amihanna is happy and confident when she's still learning a new and extremely demanding job of her own. The right clothes will help her have the confidence she needs to face her day. So, a tip, if you'll accept it?" Lorne said.

Almya lowered her hands, and the dressed dragged on the floor. She bowed her head. "Yes, of course, your majesty. I'd appreciate any tips."

He grinned, and it was his kind one. The one that made me melt just a little. He seemed to catch me mid-melt and ran a finger down my cheek before drawing me against his side. My skin was glowing, but this time I didn't care. It was just him and me here.

And Almya. He made me forget that anyone else was here with us.

Lorne gave me a wink that told me he knew exactly what he'd done, and then he focused on Almya again. "Your job isn't to put her in whatever anyone else thinks she should wear or what you think is appropriate or even what you prefer. It's not about *you*. It's about *her*. What would Amihanna feel most comfortable in? What would suit her *and* the situation? Those are questions you'll need to answer, but remember that she comes first. Okay?"

I came first?

I wasn't used to that. I was used to doing whatever I needed to survive. My needs were so much more basic. Food. Shelter. Safety. Now, I was thinking about fashion, and it was so easy to blow it off because it wasn't important. I didn't need to camouflage myself in enemy territory. Chances were that I wouldn't even have to fight in whatever I was going to wear, so I didn't have to think so practically about it either. I should just be thankful for clean clothes, let alone a closet filled with what had to be expensive pieces.

Even knowing that, I didn't want to wear a dress.

Almya chewed on her lip for a moment before standing tall again, meeting Lorne's gaze. "That is an important distinction, your majesty. I see now...I see how I've gone wrong." She turned to me, and now her smile wasn't as fake. Instead, it was smaller, calmer, and filled with an understanding I didn't see in her before. "I apologize. These dresses are similar to what some of the other High Council members wear to the meetings. I researched all night. I wanted to do a good job, but..." She glanced down at the dresses still in her hands.

Oh man. Now I felt like a real jerk. "You're doing fine. It's just... I just..." I'd said I didn't want to wear a dress so many times now that I couldn't make myself say it again.

"You can't even lie to me about it." She grinned and shook her head. "No, I wasn't doing a good job or even a fine one." She took a deep breath, and it wasn't a sigh of distress but relief when she breathed out. "But I will learn. I was trying to abide by tradition and rules, but you...you're a rebel. I haven't seen much of you. I saw you fierce and fighting on that ship and in the halls, but I don't *know* you. It's hard for me to dress someone when I don't know them, but I'm starting to see you." Her skin started to light up for the first time since I saw her, and the *fao'ana* appeared. "You should stand out. You should lean into the different because you're not hiding anymore."

She dropped the dresses on the floor and bowed deeper, fist to her chest. "Thank you, your majesty. I know what to do now. I'll have her ready straightaway."

"Good," Lorne said. "It's a treat to have the help of someone truly meant for the job."

Lorne had given her a talking-to and then left her with a sweet compliment. This is why he'd be such a good High King. He was so good it awed me sometimes.

"I'll leave you to helping Amihanna."

He brushed a way-too-quick kiss on my lips. "I'll be in our rooms."

As soon as Lorne was gone, Almya waved a hand in front of her face as if to cool herself off. "Is he always that intense?"

I couldn't help the laugh. "Yes. Pretty much."

"All right then." She turned back to the clothes. "What would she want to wear? What would *she* want to wear? What would..." She muttered to herself over and over as she moved through the racks of clothes.

When she came back, she had a pair of black pants, a pair of short-heeled booties in a dark cream color, and a flowing bright blue blouse, nearly the shade of Lorne's eyes, with long sleeves. The Aunare women didn't usually wear long sleeves to anything official, so I was confused for a second, but then I saw that the sleeves had long slits in them from shoulder to wrist. Only a small piece held them together at the elbow and then tied together at the wrist.

"Better. Much better."

Almya bowed her head as she handed over the clothes. "I'm sorry about before. His majesty was right. I was making your clothes about me, what I wanted you to wear, what I thought was appropriate, when my job is to help you look your best in something you're happy with."

I raised a brow. "So, no more dresses?"

She grinned. "No. No more dresses, unless you request it." Her tone had threads of hope woven through it.

I almost felt bad for killing that hope, but I needed to cut it or face having to disappoint her over and over. "Not happening."

For a second, I was worried she was going to stay while I changed. Thankfully, she gave me a bow and then left the room.

But then, when I finished dressing and went back into the bathroom, she was there, waiting to do my hair and makeup.

Oh boy. I was used to doing everything for myself, and now I couldn't go into the kitchens, couldn't pick my own clothes, *and* she was going to do my hair.

What the hell had I gotten myself into?

An hour later, I was both ready and extremely late.

I stepped into the living room of our suite and saw Lorne sitting on the couch with his feet propped on the massive leather ottoman, watching multiple news feeds in Aunare. More than one of them had a picture of me. I literally hadn't gone anywhere today, so I had no idea why I'd be such a hot topic. But Lorne's frequency was getting louder, more high pitched. It hadn't taken me long to figure what that sound meant.

Lorne was mad.

He was really, really mad.

The smooth, sibilant language and Lorne's anger pulled me closer to him.

I sat next to him, shoulders nearly touching, watching the screen. "What are they saying?"

Lorne was quiet for a second, and I could feel him struggling to settle down. He gave up after a second. "They still don't like you."

"Okay." They didn't have to like me.

"It's not okay." The words had more heat than I'd thought. Usually, when he was this mad, he'd be pacing and moving and unable to sit still.

It felt more dangerous that he was still right now, and I wasn't sure why or what it meant. The news looked like more of the same. So why was today different?

"I'm not offended by anything they say. It's frustrating and usually untrue, but I'm not mad." I hoped that was the right thing to say, but even if it wasn't, it was the truth. "Those reporters? They don't know me. Not really. So, what does it matter?"

"It matters that the press is now free to say what they want, and they're choosing to say this."

"Pause all media," I said, and the vid screens stopped. I needed Lorne's full attention, so I stood and tapped his legs. He dropped his feet off of the ottoman so that I could fully stand in front of him.

"Why does it matter?" I waved behind me. "Why are you so mad about it today?"

"Because." The word was bitten and angry.

That wasn't an answer. "Because why?"

"Because it's a lie. And it's not just a harmless lie. This is a big one that's hurting our ability to rally our people for the war."

He tugged his hands through his chin-length dark hair, which should've looked bad, but instead, it looked better messy. The neat and brushed look was nice, but his frustrated hair always made me smile.

But I couldn't smile. Not when he was so mad. "Okay. So, we'll fix it."

"How? You risked your life days ago to save me, to save this city, and they're still saying this stuff? I don't understand how they can't see the truth even when it's right there."

Okay. They'd been saying the same thing for days, which meant that something happened and he needed to tell me. "Why today? Why are you so mad right now?" I forced my voice to stay calm, hoping that it would balance him out a little. "What's going on?"

"My morning meeting was... not great. Worse than that, but the details aren't important. The important thing is that my call this morning made me realize that we have no hope of getting our allies to join our fight if we can't even get our own people behind us. I've been sitting here trying to figure out how to make them see, but I can't find a way."

He leaned forward, tugging on my hand until I sat next to him. "I think they're mad that you haven't given an interview yet," Lorne said. "They're thankful and polite about you saving the city in one breath, but with the next, they're questioning the viability of you as my queen. They wonder if you'd be a better consort."

"Consort?" Did that mean what I thought it meant? Because *that* wasn't any of their business.

"Meaning you'd just be my lover and not rule with me."

"Oh." That was exactly what I thought it was. "Do you want me to be your consort?" Would I be okay if that's what he really did want? I wasn't sure.

"No. If that's what I wanted, I wouldn't have asked you to rule with me. And I did. Repeatedly."

"Okay." That was good. That was much better. I'd been worried, but I didn't need to be. Not with him.

I turned my hand in his, threading our fingers together, and then looked up at Lorne. "So, who cares what they say? They're the media, but you're the High King."

"Because we need the full backing of the Aunare kings who rule our colonies and the people who hold sway over them. The other kings rule smaller populations, and they're more inclined to go along with their people's majority. They don't vote, but they hold... sway. That's the best word I can find in Earther English."

"How many kings are there?"

"Nine."

"But you're the High King?" I'd thought *High* King was a term of respect, but as usual, I was out of my depth in all things Aunare.

"Yes. My rule supersedes theirs, but again, sway comes into play. It's more than sway, though. It's not the right word at all. It's less than a vote but more than... I don't know." He let go of my hand to tug at his hair again.

He was getting frustrated, and I didn't want that. "Okay. So, what now?"

"They need to like you." He pointed to the paused vid screen. "They need to be able to see you as a leader. They need to know who you are."

I could do that. Probably. "Wasn't I supposed to give an interview?"

"Yes." He was a fraction of a frequency calmer, which meant I was helping. I just had to keep doing what I was doing. He looked at me. "It's being arranged. We're in negotiations on the questions."

Then why was this a big deal? "So, I'll do the interview soon, and everything will be okay."

"It feels as if we've already done enough to have the people's backing, but they still question you. You're gaining some in the polls, but you don't have a majority. Not even close. I don't know that an interview will make a difference. It seems like we'll need something more, but..." he took a breath. "I don't need the High Council to back me if I declare war." His voice was calmer now. "I only have to give the order. But the kings on the nine colonies can refuse to acknowledge it. They can rebuke my order."

"Why would they do that?" I didn't understand why any Aunare wouldn't want to destroy SpaceTech for what they'd done, but for another of the kings to get in Lorne's way? It just felt insane.

"My father put other kings in power that are more like him than not. He didn't want anyone forcing his hand."

I didn't know why that surprised me, but it really, truly did. Of course a weak High King would pick weaker kings. "Can you replace them?"

"Not quick enough to help us. There's a process, but it's lengthy."

"So they might act like him?"

"They might. Some of them won't, but a few... They need a majority to rebuke my order. No one king can do it."

"So, in this interview, I need to win everyone over some-how." It was a tall order, but I would do my best to figure out how to say everything that needed to be said.

"Yes."

"And you're worried that I won't?"

"I..." He winced. "Yes, but it's not about answering ques-tions the right way." His words were rushed. Each one nearly on top of the next. "I'm just not sure what an interview will do when seeing you fight in the hallways, or saving me in the concert hall, or blowing up ships in the sky didn't make a dent."

But it had made a dent. It had. I knew it because I saw the news after that. So, something changed. Something about my past made them worried about me, except Lorne was too angry

—and too worried about the war—to see through all the emotions and figure out what set them off.

If it wasn't one thing that set them off, then maybe it was a plot to keep me from ruling? Maybe some of Lorne's father's friends were acting against me?

Or maybe it wasn't as easy as either of those things. Maybe it was a combination of little things. Maybe they just didn't know me well enough to understand how I'd be as a ruler whose only promise to them was war.

Shit. It was probably the last option, which would be the hardest to fix.

Which meant I needed to figure out a way to make them understand not just me but everything at stake.

But I had no idea how.

Lorne wiped a hand down his face, and I knew he was going to try to change the subject.

"I'll take care of this," I said before I could think it through.

"What?"

"I'll make them understand who I am." I wasn't going to like it, and it wasn't going to be fun, but this was something I could do. Probably. "I'll talk to Roan about getting the interview moved up. Whatever negotiations he and Fynea are doing, I'll figure it out. If I need the kings to see me—if I need the Aunare people to understand me—then I can do that."

"I don't know how you can do more than you've already done. I don't know what you've left unsaid that could change how they feel about you. It's all there for people to watch."

He meant the footage from the attack in Ta'shena. From the attack in the estate. From their arena. From Abaddon. From the attack in the diner. They'd seen it all.

But they wanted more.

Lorne was right. I wasn't sure what else I could do or say to show them who I was, but I'd come up with something.

I liked to live in the shadows. It was where I felt comfortable.

It was how I'd survived. But it's not what I needed now. I could figure this out.

I grabbed Lorne's hand. "I'm on it. Trust me."

A line formed between Lorne's brows, and I knew he didn't trust me. He didn't know what I was going to do, which was fair. I wasn't sure what I was going to do either. But I'd figure it out. Just like I figured out everything else. That's all he needed to know.

I tugged his hand and started moving toward the door. "We have a meeting to get to, and we're already late." I hadn't gotten to eat, but I'd gone hungry before. I'd eat later.

Lorne stopped walking with me. Instead, he tugged my hand, harder than I'd tugged his. Hard enough to have me stumbling against him.

He brushed his lips against mine once. Twice. And then, the third time, he dove in. Until the room was spinning and I was out of breath and I'd forgotten everything except for the feel of him against me.

"Thank you," he said softly as he pulled away.

"What?" For the kiss? That was my pleasure, but he'd started it.

He poked a finger through my hair, putting a pin back in place. "For being you. For doing this with me. When I finally had this job, I thought that I'd be doing it alone, but it's better with you. It'll be so much better with you." He closed his eyes for a second, but when he opened them, I could nearly see his heart in them. "Thank you for accepting this job. I'm so sorry for what they're going to put you through, but everyone will be better with your help. Everything will work out." He said it with so much faith and power, and I wished I felt the same way.

I wasn't sure what I was doing, but I'd accepted my place. I wasn't sure what that meant or what I was supposed to be doing, but I'd figure it out.

I'd figure it out because failing Lorne wasn't an option.

CHAPTER FOUR

LORNE

AS WE WALKED through Rysden's estate to the High Council meeting room, I had so much I wanted to tell Amihanna, but I wasn't sure where to start. I felt like I was setting her up by taking her to this meeting without telling her specifically what it would be like or what she should say. I knew she had a packet about the council members and what they did. The basic information was there, and I didn't want to sway her thoughts or give her any predispositions against any one member. I wanted her to be who she was. I wanted her to be confident.

And yet, as we continued on our way to the meeting, I wasn't sure if I was making the right call. The note I'd received from Jesmesha this morning before my call was confusing me, and I wasn't sure I was doing the right thing anymore.

Jesmesha was one of the most respected people among the Aunare. She was tapped directly into the Goddess. and served as our prophet and guide. When Jesmesha spoke, we listened. Today, she said that I had to let Amihanna be comfortable in who she is so that she has the freedom and strength to say, do, and be exactly who she is. Only then would the Aunare truly rally behind her.

Yesterday, I wanted the Aunare to rally. After the call this morning, I needed it desperately. Jesmesha sending that note to me just before my call was exactly her style.

She was usually right, so I kept my mouth shut. I kept her advice to myself. Even if it went against every urge I had, I simply walked next to Amihanna. I had to be there to provide support and strength and that was it because I needed our people to rally behind us.

I hoped by staying silent I was letting her be her true self.

Wait a moment.

Did Jesmesha mean that I pressured Amihanna into this job? Is that what Jesmesha was saying about letting Amihanna be comfortable? That maybe I'd rushed it and should give her more time to become who she needed to be?

"Are you okay?" Amihanna broke the silence.

I stopped and looked down at her. "Yes. Why?"

"Your grip on my hand just tightened. Mind letting up a little?"

Goddess, take it. "I'm sorry." I loosened my grip and brought our joined hands up to my mouth. I gave the back of her hand a soft kiss.

"You okay?" she asked as I lowered our hands and started walking again.

"Sure." Aside from the storm of questions and doubts in my mind, I was fine.

She tilted her head at me, but didn't say anything else.

After a moment, Jesmesha's warning note tore through my mind again. If she meant that I was supposed to wait to marry Amihanna and make her queen, then she was too late. I wasn't backing down from that now. She couldn't mean that, could she?

If I was supposed to wait for Amihanna to want to be queen, why didn't Jesmesha tell me that weeks ago?

Why didn't she ever speak plainly and specifically with her bloody predictions?

And I knew the answer. Of course, I knew it. Even though we believed in following our destinies, there were still choices to be made. A person could even turn away from their destiny completely and go down an uncharted path. So, she only gave vague predictions and answers.

We passed a maid, who had paused to bow her head. I gave her a nod, so that she could keep moving on with her day.

The guards were around us, protecting us, but they knew everyone who worked in the estate. They kept track of everyone that was coming onto our property every day and the times they would arrive. If this maid wasn't supposed to be here in this hallway at this time of day, they would've moved into action.

And still, I didn't trust Amihanna's guards. The blood had been cleaned from the hallway, but I still felt it in every wall, every room, every atom of this place because it had been violated with their deceit.

We were in the process of starting to rebuild Amihanna's team, but that was going to take time.

I glanced at Eshrin, Amihanna's head guard. He would stay on, but I had questions about some of those he had set for interviews later today. Yet I knew I couldn't do everything. I had to let Amihanna handle her team, but I would question anyone who met with her approval. I needed to know her team and trust them. She was the most important person in my life, and I would do everything in my power to protect her.

There was so much against her. There was so much we needed to happen and quickly.

Goddess, please help us all. I hoped I was making the right choices.

The woman holding my hand as we made our way to the High Council meeting was everything. She was quiet today, and I knew I was as silent as she was.

I looked down at her again. Almya had put her in a lovely outfit that suited Amihanna, but also would show off her *fao'ana* when her skin brightened. The marks that showed on our skin were bright beacons that served to tell everyone who we were. The ones on the forearms showed a person's true abilities and

aptitudes. The *fao'ana* that lit on our backs showed symbols of
our past, our present, and our future. The symbols on our back
would shift and change depending on our choices in life, but
they could serve as a guide. And in Amihanna's case, they were
proof of who she truly was.

Amihanna still struggled with showing everyone her *fao'ana*,
but she was going to find that some things were easier when the
Aunare could see the marks on her skin. They wouldn't be able
to ignore the truth of her destiny when they could clearly see
them.

Her brown eyes caught mine, and I saw my future in hers.
The many versions Jesmesha had shown me. The ones where I
died, or worse—the ones where she died—they were awful and
haunting.

I saw that same haunted look in her eyes, and I wondered if it
was the future haunting them or her past.

Either way, I wanted it gone.

I paused just long enough to press my lips to hers. "You're
going to do fine. I promise."

"Right." She said the word, but it sounded like she meant the
opposite.

I wished I could make this easier for her, but the weight of
rule was heavy and there was so much that we were up against.
So much that had to happen. So many lives in the balance.

After the call this morning, I felt now more than ever that
everything and everyone was against us, and Amihanna and I
needed to be strong, united, a force to shift the fates of space and
time in our favor. If we were, then the Aunare would rally.

The Aunare needed to rally. They needed to come to terms
with the fact that we were at war and that they were going to
have to do their part. If we weren't very careful, we were all
about to meet the Goddess.

I wished I could talk to Amihanna about my call this morning, about our allies, about what Jesmesha said, but I couldn't. I
couldn't put that burden on her. Not yet. Not when she'd been

so reluctant to rule. It wasn't fair to pile everything on top of her in a matter of days. Eventually, she'd have to know how bad things truly were, but for now, I kept walking, hoping I'd have enough time to ease her into this mess we were in.

Amihanna was anxious about taking this role. With the High Council, I was giving her an easy place to start with very little risk. She needed to find her voice as a ruler, and this should do that for her and quickly. The High Council was an infuriating bunch. I was betting on the fact that she wouldn't be able to stay quiet when truly frustrated and angry with them.

I squeezed her hand. "Don't be nervous." I wanted to tell her that she had nothing to be afraid of, but those were wasted words. She would see it as a platitude and nothing more, even if it was the truth.

"You can tell?" She sounded half-horrified, half-curious. It was the horrified part that made me want to laugh.

I tugged on our joined hands so that she stumbled into me, and then wrapped my arm around her shoulders, tucking her against my side. "No one else could, but I'm your *shalshasa*." I lowered my head to whisper to her. "I can feel your mood and the tension inside you ratcheting up as we walk. There's nothing for you to be nervous about, but I know that won't mean much until you've been in front of the High Council."

Her color brightened a little, and I wasn't sure if it was my words or her nerves.

"It feels intimidating," she said finally.

It had been my words, which meant she didn't believe me. She was taking it as platitudes, just as I'd thought she would. Still, I knew I had to say it, especially when there was so much I was holding back.

"And… this is something I want to get right," she said.

Goddess. I felt that so much.

I wanted to get being her partner right. I wanted to get being the Aunare High King right. I wanted to find the right way to fight for my people, but I was pretty sure I was failing on all fronts.

I dragged my fingertips down her cheek, gaining comfort from the way her skin went even brighter with my touch. She looked at me with so much love, and I could only think of how unworthy I was for it.

"You won't get it all right. You will fail, especially at first."

She made a face, and I knew she wanted me to say something encouraging.

I wasn't sure how encouraging the truth was, but that's what I could give her. "On a good day, this is a hard, frustrating job with enormous responsibility. Since you have a passion for what you think the Aunare should do from here on out and the High Council largely disagrees, it will be even more frustrating. But I will be there with you and feeling the exact same thing, even if I can't show it. Being High King should mean that I can do, say, and feel whatever I want, but if I do that, then the people will revolt. So, it's a delicate game. One we have to play carefully."

She let out a long, heavy sigh, and I knew she was feeling the same weight of responsibility. "I'm not good at playing games like that."

"At five years old, you were the best strategist that I'd ever come across, and after everything you've gone through, you're infinitely better now. You can absolutely play games like that." I tried to think of one piece of advice that I could give her that would help and yet not interfere with Jesmesha's predictions.

Why did she send me that damned note? Wasn't this hard enough already?

I swallowed down my own frustrations. Amihanna didn't need that right now. "The High Council seems intimidating, but it's largely a safe place. Standing up in front of them and speaking is how I learned to rule. It might feel as if your father and I are throwing you in the deep end, but that's not true. It's shallow waters, and I'm with you." It was more than her father gave me, and a universe more than my father ever taught me, but I wanted to say more.

And yet, Jesmesha's message had me biting my tongue. *Again.*

Damn her.

"Any advice for me?" She looked up at me with so much hope that my heart broke open.

I wanted to say just the right thing to give her the courage she needed, and I knew I wasn't saying enough. "Speak from your heart. You are a leader. You will lead with me." I ran my fingertip down her right forearm, lighting up the *fao'ana*. "Just as your *fao'ana* says. Trust your instincts. You will know what to do."

She let out a slow breath and then turned to face the door. "Okay," she said with courage that humbled me. "Let's do this."

I nodded to Ashino—my head guard—and he opened the door. "Let's do this," I echoed her words back to her.

I believed Amihanna would be the greatest High Queen the Aunare had ever seen, but I needed her to believe it.

She didn't yet, but once she did, nothing would stand in her way.

Nothing could ever stand in her way. That was the power she wielded inside her. I just needed to stand out of her way so that she could see it.

CHAPTER FIVE

AMIHANNA

THE ROOM beyond the doorway went quiet when Ashino and Eshrin entered it. A few of our guards stayed outside with us while they cleared it. I knew I should trust all of my guards—and I did. I trusted all those I had left, but I hadn't clicked with them like I had with Eshrin. I really liked it better when Eshrin was the one to clear a room.

I waited one breath. Two. Three. And then Eshrin appeared, bowing to us.

Safe. The room was safe, and yet my nerves soared.

I'd been hoping Eshrin would say we couldn't go inside, but that hope was gone now. There was no choice but to take my first official step as the future High Queen.

Lorne squeezed me closer to his side before letting go and taking a step back. "You first."

"Great. Just throw me out the airlock. No problem."

Lorne's laugh followed me as I stepped through the doorway. Every eye was on me, and that made me want to hide. But I couldn't hide. Not anymore. Not when it was time to fight.

Eshrin and Ashino took up posts by the doors, and I moved deeper into the room with Lorne.

The High Council room was much bigger than I'd thought.

From the digital packet I read about the High Council, I knew my father used this room for any strategy sessions with his advisors as well as meeting with this council, but I'd pictured a small meeting room. I thought it was going to be something like the formal dining room with a long rectangular table and maybe some windows with a nice view of the gardens around the estate, but that was completely wrong.

There were no windows in the meeting room. Instead, the four walls were massive vid screens. Right now, they were blank white and the room was lit well, but I was sure the lights would dim if the vid screens were in use.

Today was informal, except informal felt like a lie when I looked at the massive round table that took up the center of the room. There were way too many chairs at the table, and I knew it had to be twenty-five—I'd prepared a little for this meeting, so I knew there were exactly twenty-five chairs with twenty-five people in them—but it felt like there were more. A lot more. Each chair was turned to face me and Lorne. A few of the occupants had risen to bow, but more than half stayed seated.

What did that mean? It felt like they were either insulting Lorne or me or both of us, but I didn't want to assume anything.

I glanced at Lorne, hoping for some guidance on what to do now, but he stood still. His mouth was pressed tight and I could feel him almost shaking as he held something back.

He was waiting. For what?

And then my father walked into the room, and shouted something in quick Aunare. There were mutters around the room, but nothing in Earther English. A man with graying hair rose, speaking to Rysden.

I reached up for my ear to turn on my translator and realized I'd forgotten it.

Oh shit.

"Enough," Lorne shouted. "Everyone here is to speak in Earther English out of respect to Amihanna, your future High Queen."

"If she's truly to rule us, then she should speak our language," the man with graying hair said. His words hit me hard, even though I knew it wasn't my fault. Whatever had been done to my mind to make me forget how to speak, read, understand Aunare made it next to impossible to relearn the language, but it still hurt.

It not only hurt, but it was frustrating that this man knew what happened—because *everyone* knew—and hadn't made any allowances for it. I hadn't chosen this for myself, and I couldn't fix it. This was something about me that they'd have to accept. And if they couldn't—or wouldn't—then I knew it would become a reason for them to reject me entirely as their queen.

To fail now for something that seemed so trivial was annoying and frustrating and flat-out rude.

"We've spoken about why she cannot, and I told you to welcome her today," Lorne said. His voice was flat, but I knew from the way his skin lit and his fists were clenched that he was angry. "If you choose not to respect her and everything that she has had to do—that has been done *to her*—in order for her to live, then this meeting will be cut impossibly short."

"It's our language. Our culture. If she cannot be a part of that, how can she possibly rule us?" The man sent a sharp look at me, and I didn't have an answer for it.

There was no argument to make.

Except one. "My past, my memories, and anything Aunare was wiped from me, but—" I closed my eyes for a second and let go. I let go until I felt my power filling my soul until it was seeping out my skin.

There was a quiet hum in the room when I opened my eyes again.

"I *am* Aunare. I used to speak our language. In fact, I used to prefer it over Earther English so much that even when I was running for my life, even when it would've gotten us killed, I still spoke it. That was my preference. So, my mother did what she had to do to keep us alive. I've accepted that and moved on because that's my only choice. It's in the past, and I can't change it. I worked with Jesmesha to unblock me, but whoever the doctor was that messed inside my brain did something irreversible. A lot of horrible things have happened in the last thirteen years, and if that's my biggest loss, then that's okay. Because I'm still alive. That's all that matters. It's all that *should* matter. I survived against impossible odds."

I tried to remember which council member this was, and then I knew. Councilman Vinean ni Gonean. I remembered him because his name kind of rhymed, and I thought he needed to get gone. That wasn't how his name was pronounced, but it my head, it was. Remembering that now would've made me smile, but I was staring at him and I couldn't smile.

This man was the former High King's closest friend, and while the councilman never shared the science behind the Aunare's technology, he did have a very profitable tech exchange with SpaceTech. One that skimmed just this side of traitorous.

This was one of the men that I wanted to look at carefully because he was old and powerful and I was pretty damned sure he was a very, very bad man. Judging from my first impression of him, the report was right. This man would be a problem.

"I'm doing my best to keep up, Councilman ni Gonean." I tried my best to keep any anger out of my tone, but I wasn't sure if I was succeeding. I wasn't sure I cared. "I'm not just a human or an outsider. My *fao'ana* prove that I'm Aunare enough to stand here, next to your High King, and speak to all of you. And this one here—" I tapped the zigzagging mark. Four zags and three zigs. All thick. "This one proves that I'm not dumb, not simpleminded, and it's not as if I'm unable to learn who you are." I paused, staring at Councilman ni Gonean. "Like how I learned from my reports on you that you'd like to ignore the war because of a very profitable technology trade deal you have with the Murtaghs."

He started to sputter, but I cut him off.

"I know you'd like to keep that trade going. You think I

threaten your deal because I *will* cut it off when the war starts, but what you fail to see is that my father and, much more importantly, my future husband would do the same. I've looked into anyone in this room who has had dealings with SpaceTech, and that's *all* of you. So, I know who you are. And if I were you, I'd be very afraid right now."

My father came to stand next to me. "Anyone else who believes Councilman ni Gonean is correct in his thinking should leave now and resign from your position on this council."

I wanted to tell my father that he didn't have to do that. It was too extreme to fire council members already, and if he did that, everyone would end up hating me.

But I didn't say anything because if I was going to be High Queen—and I was—and they hated me, then they needed to leave.

There was a calm in the room, but it made me uneasy, like the quiet before an explosion. It was a feeling I was used to, but I wasn't sure where it was coming from.

I scanned the room while sandwiched between my father and Lorne. I felt safe enough to study the faces of everyone here. Most had a practiced emptiness. Some looked angry or curious or something that I couldn't quite identify. But it was the empty ones and the mystery ones that worried me.

I was sure what I'd just said would get out and be turned around in the media until I was a ruler who hated the Aunare. And since my father decided to back me up on it, I was sure this was about to make life so much harder for all of us. But that didn't mean either of us was wrong for what we said or for what we would do in the coming days.

"You're in for a fight," Councilman ni Gonean said to me. His eyes were squinty and his face was red with his hatred for me. "The Aunare aren't ones to accept enemies into our midst, even if you've weaseled your way into our king's bed."

Holy shit. Had he seriously gone there?

I imagined all kinds of crazy slurs, but not *that*.

Councilman ni Gonean said something else in Aunare, and Lorne said something back with so much hate and anger in his voice that it made everything in me stand ready to fight.

I whipped around to look at him.

What had the councilman just said?

What had Lorne said back that he didn't want me to know?

I wanted to ask, but Lorne's anger was a pulsing beast. Was that the explosion? Was it his calm before the storm that I'd been feeling?

I wasn't sure, but if it was, then everyone here was in danger.

Councilman ni Gonean stormed out of the room, shouting something back in Aunare, and for once, I wished I had my translator.

Lorne said something else back, and Councilman ni Gonean froze for a second before turning to lunge at Lorne.

Oh God. Why didn't I have the stupid translator? What the hell was happening?

I saw Lorne start to move, but I was faster. I'd never seen Lorne this angry before, and I wasn't about to let him do something he'd regret.

I stepped into Councilman ni Gonean's path and shoved my palm against his chest.

He stumbled back and looked at me as if he was confused at how I got there so fast.

Did he not see what was on my skin? Had he really not watched any of the footage of me fighting? Did he think it was fake? "You're either really dumb or you have a death wish, but either way, you should leave." I poured anger into my voice, and hoped he'd run scared from this room. "*Now.*"

His eyes glanced beyond me to Lorne and widened. It was as if his mind became transparent—every thought was written on his face. Shock at what he'd said and done. Fear at what might be done to him as a result. And then he looked at me and there was anger. He wasn't afraid of me, and he probably should've been.

This man was losing his place among the Aunare, and he was blaming me for it.

Which he was welcome to do if he wanted to ignore all responsibility for his own cowardly, traitorous actions, not to mention insulting both me and Lorne.

What was he thinking with that whole *weaseled* my way into Lorne's bed thing? And in front of my father?

What an idiot.

Once he was gone and the door closed, I turned to the quiet room. Everyone watched me, waiting for me to speak. I knew that no matter what I said, some of them would still hate me. Some of them would still be angry. But if I said the right thing, maybe that would be the start of a relationship with anyone who was left.

I just hoped it would be enough.

"Well, I think this is going pretty well, don't you?" I said with a grin. It was forced and fake, but it was there.

"No." All the warmth was gone from Lorne's voice. "No, it's going terribly. I'm horrified and insulted and beyond angered by Councilman ni Gonean's words. Let's hope for all of your sakes that the tone of this meeting changes immediately."

Lorne stepped closer to the table. "This is your future High Queen. You will respect her or you will leave as Councilman ni Gonean did. *Now.*"

Oh shit.

My mind was racing, trying to find a way to calm him and fix this, but I couldn't figure out a single thing to say.

Shit.

Just *shit.*

This was going to be an awful, awkward meeting.

CHAPTER SIX

AMIHANNA

THE MEETING HAD BEEN a complete disaster. A failure of epic proportions. After Councilman ni Gonean left, it became clear that the majority of the council agreed with him. There had been screaming—by Lorne, my father, and sometimes by me—and it was ugly. It was really ugly, and I felt like I'd failed on day one.

I was trying to remember what Lorne said about how I wasn't going to be good at this at first. That I would fail. So, maybe he wasn't surprised by my performance, but I'd hoped to do better.

I'd hoped to be better.

The meeting finally died when we realized that someone in the room had been recording us. The whole thing was being live-streamed to a small group of his staff, starting with me blocking Councilman ni Gonean from lunging at Lorne. It was only then that we all finally agreed on something. Everyone was angry. The council member recording it was forced to resign his position, his devices were confiscated, and he was escorted out of the estate.

A week ago, the recording would've been spliced and cut together to make me sound awful, but now, it was just being pushed out in full, letting the people decide whose side to be on.

I wanted to see that as a good thing, but from what they were showing in the polls on the bottom of the screen, most of the viewers were on Councilman ni Gonean's side, even though what he'd said that started the argument wasn't aired.

I didn't understand why. I couldn't understand it, and I wasn't sure I wanted to.

I'd come to the gym to work off some of the anger and frustration, but I made Roan turn on the news on one of the walls. That was probably a mistake, but I couldn't turn it off.

I half-watched it as I climbed up the wall, and then Councilman ni Gonean's face came on the screen as he sat next to the reporter.

"What the hell? He's there in person now?"

"Want me to turn it off yet?" Roan yelled up at me. "You don't need to watch this junk. It's not good for you."

"No. Leave it. I want to see what he's going to say." I stopped climbing halfway up the wall so that I could read the subtitles.

I didn't need to stop for long. Apparently, I was an alien coming in to their world, starting a war, costing everyone money and possibly their lives, and all because I'd fucked their king. At least that's what the councilman believed.

I started moving again.

"Don't listen to him," Eshrin said from where he climbed beside me.

It was probably bad that I hadn't noticed Eshrin coming up the wall.

"He's an old, angry man who's afraid of losing money and power. That's not about you. That's about him."

Maybe Eshrin had a point, but the station was running a poll at the bottom of the screen. I glanced over. "Seventy-two percent agree with him."

"And according to their extremely inaccurate polling, twenty-eight agree with you. Only a small percentage of their viewers call in, and it's always more negative than positive."

I shook my head and started moving again. "I don't know if

you know this, but seventy-two is *a lot* more than twenty-eight, even with crappy polling."

"And twenty-eight is more than two which is where you started in their polling when you first got here."

I paused when I reached the top to soak that in. "It was really that low?"

"It was. You just need time."

That was the problem. "I'm not sure how much time we have."

"When time runs out, it'll be because it's apparent that we are at war, and then you'll be at the overwhelming majority approval that you want."

"Maybe." I let that soak in as I let go from the wall, flipping to the floor.

Eshrin landed beside me.

"It's still insulting."

"Of course. Your anger is well placed, but we'll use it up today."

I glanced at the screen and then back at him. "You sure you're up for that? I'm pretty angry right now."

Eshrin's answering grin was a little evil, a little goofy, and told me he was more than ready for a fight.

I laughed and turned to the wall. "One more time."

"I'll grab the *faksano*."

Yes. I loved that particular Aunare weapon the best. The *faksano* were two, short bo staffs that could be charged with my power and act as a focus when I used my ability. Practicing with them had become one of my favorite things. "Thanks." I was going to need the work out because if I stopped moving, I'd want to hunt down that idiot councilman and kill him.

But I couldn't kill him. I had to be *diplomatic*.

I wasn't sure why the Aunare were buying his line of crap.

I'd told them again and again and again what had happened on Earth. Why weren't they ready for a fight? Why weren't they aching to destroy SpaceTech?

I didn't understand. It didn't compute. It went against all logic.

"Am," Roan called up to me.

I hung from a hand grip fiftyish feet up in the air and glanced down at him. He was sitting on the bench behind the half-wall of the gym. The rest of the viewing area was thankfully empty because we'd asked everyone to leave.

"What?" I asked.

"Are you almost done? Because we've got shit to do." He waved his tablet at me. "Your schedule is packed."

It might be packed, but I was doing the most important thing right now. "Cancel everything." I didn't know what "shit" he had for me to do, but I wasn't doing anything but this. I was riding a very fine edge. The power inside me was growing, and I hadn't fully figured out how to control it yet. If someone pissed me off, there wasn't a guarantee I wouldn't turn them into ground bits of flesh and blood.

Didn't he see how on edge I was? My skin was seconds away from flickering with need for a release of my powers.

"You need to breathe," Eshrin said from the floor below me. His darker skin was lit, but not as bright as mine. Not because it couldn't match mine, but because he was in control of his powers. Something I lacked, big time.

Eshrin had passed every test to become one of the most elite class of warriors among the Aunare—a royal guard. He was strong, observant, trained in every weapon and every type of warfare imaginable, and yet today, he wasn't using any of those elite guard skills. Right now, he was trying to help me figure out how to calm down.

"Focus." Eshrin whacked the *faksano* together. "Breathe."

"I'm trying." But the harder I tried, the less control I had. I needed Lorne, but he was busy and he was quickly becoming a crutch. I needed to figure this out for myself.

I made my way to the next grip. Two more to the top. I reached those with my next breath, and then I used my legs to push away from the wall. I leaped away and flipped down to the ground.

Eshrin walked over to me. "You can't see the meeting as a failure. Don't let those people rip control from your hands. This will work out. You're meant to lead us. We know it. We can see it." He motioned to my arms, and then to my back.

"They don't seem to agree." I mimicked his motion, except toward the vid screen. The sound was off now, but the Earther English subtitles ran in shining gold text with a black shadow to make it feel as if it was popping out from the screen.

I read two words of it before turning away. "Tell me something else. Give me something else to focus on."

Eshrin handed me one of the *faksano*. "I have three more guards for you to interview. They were on the schedule that you just had Roan cancel."

Now that was something. I took the *faksano* from him, and glanced around the room, counting my guards. There were three others with us in the gym, which meant that I was five on-duty guards short.

There were two guards sleeping right now, which made for a total of six guards. I was supposed to have nine on duty at all times with a minimum of nine more off duty. Lorne wanted me to have twenty-seven, but he was insane with that number. I got why he needed so many, but I wasn't that important. At least not yet.

My guards were supposed to be on a half-day schedule, six days a week. But right now they were taking only a quarter of a day to sleep before jumping back on duty and having no days off. They all rotated throughout the day, but Eshrin was on duty all day except for five hours when he knew I was sleeping. That's all the time he would take off, and I was pretty sure he only did that because he knew he'd get weaker if he didn't sleep.

My guards were going to burn out if we didn't accept more, but Eshrin was being extremely picky.

Komae—the guard that tried to assassinate me—had been

not just his second in command, but his best friend. After that betrayal, we'd put all my guards on probation. Except for Eshrin. He'd proven himself and I'd clicked with him. I trusted him as much as I could trust anyone.

The rest of my guards were given a few days to prove their ability and dedication to me as a guard. Now only six had passed onto full duty.

But now that the media was fully against me again, I was sure the faction of extremist Aunare would pick back up on their attempts to kill me, which meant I needed more guards.

"When did you want to interview them?" If the interviews could wait until I wasn't so angry, I'd make it work.

Eshrin stared at me for a moment. "Whenever you think you're calm enough to handle it? I can have them wait."

"Calm?" I laughed. "So, never? Does never work?"

"Come on now." He twirled the *faksano* slowly, almost as if the move were rote. Which made sense. "The meeting wasn't that bad."

I raised a brow at him. "Were we in the same meeting?"

"It was a disaster," Roan yelled from where he was sitting on the stands. "And now you're pissing off more people because you're not showing up to another meeting. You're lucky I love you."

"Better that they're pissed off than dead."

Eshrin chuckled, his gray eyes glittering. "You're not that bad off. I keep telling you that you won't lose control."

He sounded so sure, but I wasn't. I wasn't at all. "You don't know that."

"I do because if you were going to lose control, you would've killed Councilman ni Gonean the second he said—" Eshrin didn't say the rest, which was smart, especially with the way my skin started flashing.

"He's an idiot," Roan yelled over to me. "And scared."

"Scared," I muttered. "That feels like a way to excuse whatever he said."

"What did you say?" Roan asked. "I couldn't hear you."

"Nothing," I said. "It's fine."

"Oh shit." Roan let out a whistle.

"What?" Eshrin asked.

"Am only says something's fine when she wants someone dead."

I turned to face Roan in the stands. He was grinning like an idiot, but when I glanced back at Eshrin, he looked curious.

"Don't listen to him." I turned back to Roan. "You're making it sound like I killed people left and right on Earth, and I didn't. I didn't even kill Jason Murtagh when he—"

"You should've," Eshrin said next to me. His voice was cold, maybe even colder than when he talked about Komae. "You really should have."

I glanced at him, and I knew he was right. If I had, maybe I wouldn't have ended up on Abaddon, but if I started down that road, killing people I didn't like, I wasn't sure where I'd end-up. "I agree. Hindsight. But I didn't know who he was and—"

"Not because he's leading SpaceTech against us. Because of what he did to you. What he did in that diner—"

Suddenly I was back there.

His fat fingers on me.

In me.

I dropped the *faksano* and ran full speed at the wall before I could hear the end of Eshrin's sentence.

I didn't want to think about what happened in the diner.

Or what happened after.

I was here. I was safe. I had Lorne.

I was safe.

I had Lorne.

But now that he'd said it, I was back there. In that diner. The anger. The violation. The hate. It was all there burning inside of me as if it had just happened.

I hit the top of the wall, and then flipped to the floor.

Went up the wall. Down to the floor.

Up the wall. Floor.

Wall. Floor.

I didn't know how many times I'd done it before I noticed someone beside me. Someone not Eshrin. Someone that was trying to balance my control.

Lorne.

I looked over and my hand slipped.

His hand snatched my wrist before I could fall uncontrolled to the ground. "You with me yet?"

I panted for a second before I could find enough air to answer him. "When did you get here?"

"Twenty minutes ago. I tried talking to you, but you didn't hear me. Your mind wasn't here."

I swallowed. "I'm here now."

Lorne glanced beyond me. "You'll catch her."

"Yes, your majesty. I have her."

Lorne let me go, and I fell. Half a breath and then I was in Eshrin's arms. I looked into his stormy gray eyes. I wasn't sure what I saw in them. I trusted Eshrin, but I was still getting to know him. Something about the look in his eyes worried me.

Eshrin studied me for a second before he put me on my feet, stepping back and bowing. "My deepest apology. I spoke out of turn, and—"

"It's not your fault, Eshrin." It really wasn't. My flashbacks and anger were so much less than they had been, but were still there. Brewing. Simmering. Any little thing could make the anger boil over until I was ready to explode. "It feels... fresh sometimes, but that's not your fault."

"It is." He pressed his fist to his heart and bowed his head a little lower, still not meeting my eyes. "I will step down from my position—"

What? No. "Don't be stupid. We clicked. You're stuck with me now. Just like Roan is." I pointed at Roan where he was sitting.

"Yep." Roan backed me up just like he was supposed to as he walked over to us. "It's a forever kind of thing for her. I keep trying to shake her loose, but look at me now. Managing her schedule like a chump."

I glanced over at Roan, but he was grinning. He gave me a cocky wink, and I couldn't help but roll my eyes. I loved the idiot, and he loved me. He was happy with his job, and actually, he was pretty good at it, too. He'd been taking care of me for years on Earth.

Lorne landed next to us, and I looked up into his eyes. The aquamarine color had depths that I was only just learning. Right now, it was dark with worry. "Scared me," he said.

I put my hand on his cheek.

He lowered his lips to mine—a simple tiny touch that was there and gone. The feel of it eased the hold anger had on my soul for a second, and I needed more.

This. This was what I needed to feel.

I ran my fingers through his hair and pulled him down for another kiss. A deeper one. One that made my breath stall, my heart race, and my soul beg for more.

The gym faded away along with everything else in my mind, until there was no room for anything else. It was just the feel of his lips on mine. His tongue against mine. His hands—one holding me tight while the other ran up and down my spine, spreading heat through my body until I was sure I was burning.

I needed to be closer to him.

I started tugging at his shirt, but it wasn't coming off fast enough.

And damn him. Why was he wearing a shirt? He always took it off to train.

"Are you guys seriously doing this right now?"

Roan's voice had me freezing, with my hands still gripped in Lorne's shirt, a half of a second away from ripping it from his body.

Instead of ripping it, I tugged a little so that my forehead rested against Lorne's bare chest.

"You do realize that you're still in a room. With people.

Multiple people. Including *me*." Roan was making this so much worse, and he was right.

Damn it. I was in a room full of guards, and I'd forgotten about them. How was that even possible?

I looked up at Lorne, but he didn't seem embarrassed. If anything he looked amused and maybe a bit smug.

"You were going to let me rip your clothes off here. In front of everyone?" I whispered to him while wishing death from embarrassment was a thing. It was just my guards, a few of his, and Roan in the room, but was he for real?

"The guards have their backs turned." He motioned for me to look.

He was right. They were all against the wall now, facing it, backs to whatever happened in the center of the room—even Eshrin.

"They would've politely ignored it and never mentioned it to us, each other, or anyone else. That's what they're trained to do. My father was always afraid of assassination, so he never was alone. Never. His guards were with him *everywhere*."

"Gross. Seriously? Why would he want that?"

"I think he actually preferred it."

Every time I learned something new about that man, I liked him less.

"Roan was the only unknown factor in this room, and I would've put money that he'd run away in disgust." Lorne said the last bit louder.

"I almost did," Roan yelled back. "So, if you could keep your *business* in your rooms that would make everything better."

"Shut it," I yelled back at my best friend, but I couldn't look away from Lorne. His hair was a little messy and his cheeks were flushed. Not from the workout, but from what I'd done to him. "I missed you this morning."

"I'm sorry. I had an early meeting." He gave me his small smile, the one that held a promise for something more when we were alone.

I wanted that. I wanted more time with him without guards and meetings and talks of war and strategy. I wanted so much of him, and I knew that there wasn't time now. This great pulsing need in my heart and soul for him would never be fully quenched, not ever. So, for now, I would have to wait.

Tonight. Tonight would be different. Tonight I would be alone with him and that would have to be enough.

I dropped his shirt, smoothing it out. "How did the rest of the meeting go?"

His grin faded away, and what remained was annoyance that showed in the crease between his brows. "I left shortly after you did, and then I had some other meetings. They were frustrating. So, I needed to train just as much as you did."

I hated that for him. I hated that I was making his life harder. I hated that the Aunare weren't accepting me like he wanted, but I wasn't sure how to change their minds.

I wasn't sure what I could do to make them see that the war wasn't my fault or how to make them understand if they didn't already see the truth. I told Lorne I'd find a way to win them over, but I hadn't had time to think about how to make that happen.

I needed a quiet moment to figure that out. Maybe with Roan or even my father. There would be a way to make it happen. I just had to find it.

I needed to find a way to gain the Aunare's support if we were going to win this war. And we had to win. SpaceTech had to be destroyed. Not just because they were a danger to the Aunare, but the Earthers—those on Earth and those on the colonies—needed freedom from their tyranny. And if the Aunare went down, there was literally no other force that would stand in their way. Within this next decade—maybe two—SpaceTech would own the universe.

I was sure the allies would think I was nuts if I told them that. There was no way they'd believe it. The universe was such a vast space, but they were greatly underestimating the greed and evil that was SpaceTech.

So, how could I make them see?

I had to find a way or everything would be lost.

"Want a quick spar?" I asked him.

He looked over his shoulder at Ashino, his head guard, and gave a nod. "Actually, that sounds really good," he said to me.

Eshrin picked up our abandoned *faksano* sticks and tossed them to us.

I spun one in my hand a few times before looking up at Lorne. "Things might be crazy and they might get worse, but I'm thankful that we can have some fun mixed in."

Lorne's quick flash of a smile was the kind that made my heart jolt. It was happy and free and full of love. He stalked over to me, gripped my *faksano* and gave it a quick jerk until I tumbled into him. "I love you, Amihanna."

Four words and I was gone. But that last one—my name—in that tone of his...

My skin was bright. Brighter than when I'd been angry and my mind had been full of the past and ready to explode, because this time it wasn't something bad that brought my power to light. This time it was good. The best kind of good.

It was love.

Lorne was my partner, my love, my life. And apparently my *shalshasa*. I was still figuring out what the last one meant, but whatever it meant, I liked it.

When we started sparring, it was with that love in our hearts and passion in our moves.

And it was fun.

I might not have had the easiest life on Earth, but surviving had been worth it.

For moments like this, every bit of pain and hunger and anger had been worth it. I'd do it all again. For him, I would do anything.

Even rule.

CHAPTER SEVEN

AMIHANNA

I'D BEEN HAVING way too much fun sparring when Lorne got pulled away for yet another meeting. Somehow working out didn't feel as much fun, so I called it a day and went to shower and grab food. Except Plarsha kicked me out of the kitchens. Again.

Lame.

But I noticed some of the looks from the cooks at the prep stations, and they legitimately looked uncomfortable with me being in their workspace. Seeing discomfort on their faces told me that this was something I was going to have to give up, but it was hard to let go. There were so many times that I'd had to beg for food or grab it out of the trash or worse—starve.

When Mom finally got the job at the diner, we had food. For a while, I just got her leftovers, but once I started waitressing, I always had a meal there. Abaddon had some food, but it was awful and synthetic.

Since I'd arrived on Sel'Ani, I'd gotten used to having the ability to grab food for myself whenever I wanted, however much I wanted. But now I had to let go and trust that they'd provide for me. It was also a big shift for me to be in charge of every aspect of my life then handing over big chunks of that control.

But I had to.

So, instead of fighting with Plarsha about how I should stay, I apologized and told them thank you for all their hard work. And then I left.

Which meant I was now stuck with eating in the informal dining room off the kitchen for every meal. At least I wasn't in the formal one. The one with a milelong table and stiff chairs and no windows. This one was much more comfortable with windows and light and chairs covered in thick cushions on the seat and back. It was only weird because I wasn't used to eating at a dining table so often. I'd come here a few times to eat with Roan and Lorne, but now this was where I'd take every single meal. Unless I ate in my room, which was another option. Honestly, anything but the formal dining room would do.

When I got to the informal dining room, Roan was sitting there waiting for me. A few minutes later, my parents showed up.

I gave him a look and he shrugged.

He'd noticed the distance between me and my mom. It wasn't our normal, and I knew he was trying to fix it, but there wasn't really anything to fix. She was busy and so was I. But I guessed having a meal with my parents wasn't a bad thing.

The food started coming almost immediately. Platters of things I knew and some that were strange. After a few completely disgusting bites, Roan and I turned it into a game. It was a combination of daring each other to try new foods, and if it turned out to be something gross, trying to trick the other one into eating it. We called it Gross or Good.

From the look on my father's face, I wasn't sure if he was annoyed or amused or both.

I spooned up a hunk of something swimming in a green sauce and took a bite. My first urge was to spit it out and down a big bite of bread from the basket in the center of the table, but then Roan would for sure not try it. He had to suffer with me. What kind of friend would I be if I deprived him of such a character-building experience?

The worst part was the green sauce. It tasted sour and slimy, and I hadn't been expecting either. At least that's what I thought until I bit down on the hunk of whatever was swimming in the sauce. The chewy thing somehow slipped from between my teeth, and I could've sworn it was wiggling.

I held it on my tongue and it wiggled again.

I stifled a gag.

Nope. No. No. The sauce was *not* the worst part. Not even a little bit.

"No." Roan started laughing. "I know that face. Your eyes are watering. You can't cover that up. It's fucking gross and I'm not trying it. Gross. Final vote."

I would've tried to convince him it was actually good, but I couldn't.

I reached for my napkin and spit it out while grabbing my water glass with the other hand. As soon as it was out, I downed the water to keep from throwing up.

It wasn't helping.

"Bread. Bread. Bread." I reached for the bowl. "Don't throw up. Don't throw up," I muttered as I frantically shoved more and more bread into my mouth.

My father laughed loud and full.

I froze mid-chew and looked up at him. Was he crying?

Was my father laughing so hard at me that he was *crying*?

My mother slapped his shoulder. "Stop it, Ry."

"My apologies," he said through his fit of laughter. "I wish I could help it, but it was just too funny." And the jerk just kept right on laughing. "I can't believe you ate that."

"Great. Next time I nearly throw up, I'll aim your way." I swallowed the bread and immediately shoved another bite in my mouth. "I was leaning toward you being annoyed with me and Roan," I said around the food.

"What?" That had him sobering. "Why?"

I swallowed and tried to figure out why it wasn't obvious. "Because we were making a game of trying out food that I think I'm supposed to like."

"Oh, no one likes *nic'natarani*." He grinned. "I think the kitchen staff must be talking about your game in the back and they're having a bit of fun with you now."

My mouth dropped open. "You're kidding." They would do that?

"No." His cheek twitched and I got the feeling that he was trying not to laugh again and about to fail. "I'm not."

"I... I thought this was all part of my Aunare education." I waved to the thirty or so platters that had been shoved onto the table, covering almost every inch of it.

He cleared his throat, but it sounded like it was smothering a laugh. "You could say that." His voice was a little higher than normal. "*Nic'natarani* is an adopted Aunare dish, from one of our colony planets, Shet'malan. It's a traditional dish from the native people there, and a bit of an acquired taste."

Shet'malan? He had to be joking. "It's not even an Aunare dish?"

"No. No. That worm—"

I threw my hand over my mouth as I gagged. "Worm?" The word was more whimper than anything, but I had to ask.

"Yes. I'm afraid so—" He lost it then, laughing hard.

"You ate worms." Roan was cracking up so hard I could barely make out the words.

I would've given him shit but I was too busy trying not to throw up. I downed another piece of bread and then gulped water, trying not to think about it too hard.

"Technically I didn't eat it." I said when I was pretty sure I wasn't going to vomit. "And I spit it out, you jerk." I balled up the napkin—the one still warm and wet with the wriggling worm inside of it—and threw it at Roan.

Who batted it away.

The napkin hit the table and flew open, revealing the half-chewed worm, which then wiggled again.

Roan screamed like a little girl. "Some of that green shit is on my hand!"

Everyone in the room—my parents, the guards, the staff waiting to take away plates—started laughing.

I couldn't help but join in. "All of you are a bunch of assholes. I'm going to remember that no one—not one of you in this whole room—said a word while I almost ate a living *worm*." I reached for the platter of *ra'altan*. Lorne's sister, Nori, had been keeping me supplied with her famous pastry. We'd been saving it for dessert, but now it was mine. "And for that, I'm not sharing this."

"Oh, come now, my daughter. Don't be mean." My father said the words, but he was wiping tears from his eyes.

I hugged the plate. "Mean? You want to talk about mean. Just look at that worm." I pointed a finger at the nasty thing on the crumpled napkin.

That set off another wave of laughter.

I bit into my delicious pastry. They could laugh all they wanted, but I still wasn't sharing. Especially when there was still a slight aftertaste of worm in my mouth.

One of the kitchen staff slipped into the room holding a mug.

I narrowed my gaze at her. "You guys are all mean."

She tried not to smile, but I'd spent too much time in the kitchens before they kicked me out for her to take me seriously.

"*Wyso.*"

"If you think this will make up for worms—" I had another idea. "Maybe I should be let into the kitchens to see—"

"No, Amihanna," my mother said. "It's not right."

I glanced at her. "I'm going to rule. I should get to decide where I can go and—"

My mother cleared her throat, and I knew what she meant. She wanted me to stop talking.

"Okaaay." I drew out the word so that she'd know I got it.

She didn't need to make a thing of it. "I wouldn't want to make anyone *uncomfortable* by grabbing whatever I want from the kitchen." I took the *wyso* from the kitchen maid. "What's your name?"

"Sayalin."

"Thank you, Sayalin."

She pressed her fist to her heart before leaving.

"You sure you don't want to try that last dish?" My father pointed to a bowl that had a number of unidentifiable objects floating in a watery brown sauce.

I narrowed my gaze at him. "No. Especially not after you mentioned it."

He gave the tiniest of tiny pouts, so small I almost thought I'd imagined it. "You don't trust me?"

I gave him a look, and then I carefully pushed the bowl closer to him. "You first."

He started laughing again, and I knew he'd joined our game of Gross or Good.

This was the first nice meal I'd had with my father. Actually, it was the first meal. We'd been in the dining room at the same time before, but never for long and not like this—from start to finish of a meal, with chitchat and laughing. If someone had told me I'd be sitting here having a good time with my father today, I'd have thought they were crazy.

But I was sitting here, having a meal—a family meal—with him and it wasn't awful.

This was a side of my father that I hadn't seen before. Who knew he could even laugh, let alone laugh like that? With his whole body and tears and bending over as he slapped a hand on the table.

My mother had even cracked a grin. Her gaze darted back and forth between us, and then she settled back in her chair.

I could almost see her thoughts, that this was how our family was supposed to be. How it would've always been if we hadn't been separated. Her satisfaction with me and my father having fun together was something so thick and tangible that I could almost hold it in my hands.

The door whooshed open, and my father's laughter cut off. All the fun was gone, and instead, I was instantly looking at the version of my father that I was used to.

It was almost like Lorne and his king face, and I wondered if my father was the one to teach him that trick. It was one that I should learn—because that would come in handy—but I hated that they could both do it.

I twisted in my chair to see who had caused such an extreme shift in my father and saw Captain ni Eneko entering the room.

He gave my father a quick bow before pulling out the chair beside me and sitting. He placed his tablet face down on the table and turned to me.

If the sitting next to me didn't clue me in, the way he was looking at me did.

I gave a quick glance to Roan—asking him if he knew what was going on without actually saying anything. That was the joy of having my best friend around. I didn't need words for him to understand me.

He gave me a slight shake of the head and then a shrug. That was his way of saying *I have no idea, but we should hear him out.*

I gave him a nod back, and then turned to Captain ni Eneko. "Are you just hungry or ..."

"Or."

I took a breath, preparing for whatever came next. "What's happened now?"

"Nothing yet, but I think I might have found a SpaceTech cell."

"And you haven't contacted me?" my father cut in.

"No, sir. I wanted Amihanna to confirm it for me, and I'd love her advice on how to handle them. The last group we captured—"

"All self-terminated," my father finished for him.

"What?" The word had more of a slap to it than I wanted, but I couldn't help it. "You're joking."

"No. I'm not sure how. We did get to question a few for a bit before, but—" Captain ni Eneko looked at my father. "She has more knowledge of SpaceTech than either of us, and there's something I'm missing. I'd like these spies—if they truly are SpaceTech—to be captured *and* questioned."

He had my full attention.

Captain ni Eneko placed his hand on the tablet and pressed his lips tightly together, as if he was thinking through what he wanted to say. "I'm not certain. I want you to look at the footage, and then ideally, I need to train a team to find them. I can't tell like you can, and I know I won't always be able to come to you."

"Let's not worry about that. I'm here. I can help. And I can help while training a team, if that's what you want. But what makes you think this group you found is a cell?"

"It's a feeling I get. Nothing more. Nothing that gives me the authority to enter someone's residence. The people in the city are too on edge for me to not be certain without a doubt that I have the right person, and I just don't have that level of certainty."

I held out my hand for his tablet. "Footage, please."

He placed it in my hand. I watched for what felt like too long, but I didn't see anyone with the trademark SpaceTech walk. No sign of the way SpaceTech trained its people to move and scan their surroundings.

I wasn't sure what had set off the captain's gut, but I was pretty sure there was nothing here.

I started to shake my head, but then something caught my eye. "This one." I paused the video and pointed out a woman. "She's SpaceTech."

Captain ni Eneko sighed. "That wasn't even one of the people I'd thought. How—" He stood and faced my father. "I'm failing you. I'm failing our people. I don't have the ability to keep our city safe. I'm formally stepping down as—"

"Absolutely not." My father cut off Captain ni Eneko's resignation before he could finish. "You're doing more than what you were trained for, and you'll learn with my daughter's help. I'll not hear of a resignation until you've completed whatever training my daughter decides you need to her satisfaction." My father's command left no room for negotiation. "Understood?"

"Yes, sir." The captain sat down again. "How did I miss this woman? What am I doing wrong?" He replayed the footage. "I don't understand. I've been trying to learn, but I failed."

"You didn't fail. You did have a SpaceTech operative on the footage you showed me. That gut feeling you had was right. Something was wrong, just not what you thought. Your gut just needs a little tweak." I replayed the footage again.

He shook his head. "How do you even see it?"

"First off, who did you think was SpaceTech?" That started off a discussion.

My father circled around the table and took the tablet. He put the footage on one of the walls, and then we went over who he thought might be SpaceTech. Roan, my mom, and I pointed out why he was wrong. I'd forgotten how good my mom was at this, until she piped up to add in what she looked for—which was mostly about the shoulders and hands. That wasn't what I usually paid attention to, but she was right.

We studied the woman frame by frame. When we were done, both the Captain and my father looked more confused and frustrated then when we started.

"Will you help me?" Captain ni Eneko asked with more than a touch of desperation. "I cannot abide SpaceTech spies in my city. I cannot sleep until they're gone."

I looked up at my father. I wasn't sure what I was allowed to do or what I was supposed to do. All I knew was that I failed at the High Council meeting. He gave a tiny nod. At least this was something I could do.

"You in?" I asked Roan.

"Patrolling with you? Hell yeah. You know it, babe." He grinned. "It'll be like old times."

"Shouldn't you discuss it with Lorne?" my mother asked. "It sounds like it could be dangerous. I'm not sure it's wise."

I guessed maybe I should've discussed it, but I wasn't going to. I knew that I wouldn't be able to do patrol forever. This was going to be something that I could do in my off time while I learned what I was actually supposed to be doing.

But training the Aunare police to hunt down SpaceTech's spies was a good use of my time. This was helpful. This I could actually do and do it well.

I might be new to this queen job, but this seemed to fill at least some part of it—protecting my people. Lorne couldn't be mad about that, could he?

No.

Or, at least I didn't think he would be.

CHAPTER EIGHT

AMIHANNA

AFTER I ARRANGED to meet Captain ni Eneko in the morning, I interviewed three possible guards with Eshrin. Two I liked. One was a hard pass. But that was progress. I was going to have to build the team slowly, even if that was frustrating for everyone else. I hated that I passed on the last one—we *needed* every guard we could get—but something about him... I couldn't put it into words, but even just the mention of hesitation to hire him had Eshrin hauling the poor guy out of the room.

Hauling might've been too strong of a word. It was more of a hustle out and then a guarded escort to the gates. I was pretty sure Eshrin was overreacting, but after Komae, I couldn't really blame him.

The other two guards were going to have to go through a second interview with my father and Lorne for final approval, and then—if all went well—they'd start the day after.

I wanted to believe that I didn't even need any guards, but if last week taught me anything, it was that I did need them. This was my life now. Everything was changing.

Everything. The quicker I came to terms with it, the better off I'd be.

After the interviews, I went back to the suite I shared with

Lorne, and thought about wandering into the kitchens—I was hungry, and I wanted payback for the worm—but Lorne was there waiting for me. He wanted us to go out. On a date. A real, legit date.

I'd never gone on a date, and I was sure if he'd given me time to think about it, I might've been nervous. But I wasn't. I wasn't anything except excited to spend time with him and not worry about him running off to another meeting.

I hadn't left the estate since the attack on Ta'shena, so I didn't even question where we were going or why or what. I was just happy to sit and chat with Lorne. We weren't even talking about anything important like the news or the war, but instead, he was telling me about a bracelet that could store power, kind of how the *faksano* did, and then it could be used later. He thought it could be useful to me, and honestly, it sounded too good to be true. And a cheat. But maybe it was okay to cheat a little bit, especially when it meant the people around me would be safe while I figured out how to control my power.

It wasn't until we were approaching our destination that I realized where we were going, and then I got excited. Really, truly excited.

The ship started to slow, and I rose from my seat next to Lorne, eyes wide, taking in the view. I stepped closer to the massive vid screen on Lorne's Sel'Ani transport ship.

The first time I'd seen Ra'mi—Ta'shena's largest market— had been on a vid screen. I'd been in awe and that had just been footage from street cameras. In person, I wasn't sure what I thought. I couldn't think. I didn't even know how to process what I was seeing.

The market was in the center of five buildings, spanning multiple levels, but that wasn't what stood out. It was that each level was made of glowing light. I could see Aunare actually walking on beams of light. I knew there was floor there—I knew it had to be there—but I couldn't *see* it.

Magic. It had to be some kind of Aunare magic.

"It's pretty, right?" Lorne said from beside me.

I couldn't look away from the market. *"Beautiful.* Please tell me we're getting out here." I had to walk around on those floors. I wanted to feel what it was like to walk on light.

"We're getting out here." His voice was soft and happy and I always wanted it to be like that.

I glanced at him and saw the joy in his eyes, and then to our guards. Tonight, I had all of my guards here with me, plus nearly two dozen of Lorne's guards—which was only a quarter of his total guards. He had a lot more than me, and not just for now. For always. When I'd asked why, it was because he left the estate more often. He needed a bigger pool to pull from, and now I understood why.

It would be a long day for my guards, and a tired guard wasn't a good guard.

If we could've left my guards at the estate and taken more of Lorne's guards with us, that would've been fine with me. But my guards protected me above anyone. Lorne's would protect him. Their jobs didn't always align. I was okay with the risk, but Lorne wasn't.

By tonight, my guards were going to be exhausted, but we had enough to cover us from any angle. The market and its levels of light didn't leave a lot of places for us to hide. If someone wanted to come after us, this would definitely be the place to do it.

"Ra'mi has always been one of my favorite places," Lorne said. "Not just for the food, but to be around the everyday Aunare who are living their lives. Being here helps keep everything in perspective. Otherwise, it can be easy to lose sight of the people that matter. Those we're responsible for."

Those we're responsible for. That seemed like such a heavy statement as I looked out at the crowds—such a small percentage of our people—that I wasn't even sure if I could process it.

Was I up for the job?

Would the Aunare let me stick around long enough to find out?

"Be honest—are you mad about the meeting today?" I asked him, even if I was a little scared of the answer.

Lorne looked down at me and studied me for a second as if to see if I was truly asking. "Of course I am." He sounded a little confused about why I'd ask, but I had to know for sure.

I'd been worried about that, but I thought I'd have to pry the truth from him. I didn't think he'd just tell me instantly that he was mad at me.

Unless he wasn't mad at me. "Are you angry with how I did?" I needed to be sure. There was a lot that happened at the meeting.

"No. Amihanna." Now he didn't just sound confused. He sounded shocked that I'd thought it. "*No*. Never at you."

I let go of the breath I'd been holding.

Lorne pressed his lips together as he thought, and then he nodded. "I wasn't going to tell you, but I think you need to know that the High Council is... it'll be a place for you to learn how to rule, and that's it. You don't need to censor yourself with them or worry if you lose your patience with them. Just be you and everything will fall as it should."

"I did that this morning and it turned out great." I laid on the sarcasm thick and gave him a forced smile.

He shrugged as if the disaster today was no big deal. "It was always going to be a rough start, but it's a start. That's the important thing."

I wished I could feel that optimistic about it, but I was too much of a realist. I wasn't sure he could promise me that the Aunare would ever accept me, and I couldn't really promise to make them. That wasn't how ruling worked, at least not in my experience. Because that's exactly what SpaceTech did, and that wasn't anything I wanted to emulate.

"I can feel you thinking, and that's not what I want. At least not thinking about whatever you're thinking right now." Lorne stared down at me. "Is there anything about the meeting that's worrying you in particular?"

I shook my head, but then I thought of something. "What did he say? In Aunare? Before you kicked—"

Lorne grew bright and he closed his eyes. "You can ask me a lot of things, and if you press me, I'll answer. But I don't want to answer that. *Please* don't make me say it. Know that he said something awful about you, and I won't hurt you by repeating his words."

I reached up and cupped his cheek, tapping it a little so that he'd open his eyes. "I won't—"

"Yes. You would, and you'd have every right to ask for his life once you knew. No one should ever say anything like that to you."

Holy shit. Whatever that jerk had said must've been awful.

And now I really, *really* wanted to know. "Please tell me what—"

"You don't want to know," a voice said from behind me.

I looked to see who had spoken. Ashino, Lorne's head guard, rarely ever spoke to me. That he had meant whatever was said, it had to have been truly terrible.

Okay. I had to know. I was going to make him tell me. "It's not like this doesn't concern me. It's about *me.* I can't have everyone know except for *me.* The meeting is mostly on the news, and I can—"

"No, you can't. I made sure you'd never accidentally find out what was said." The ferocity of Lorne's voice took me by surprise. "I'm the High King. I have that power, and I used it today. "

What? "How?"

"It's why I left the meeting right after you did. My team tracked down the people who had access to the video. I made sure that what the *former* councilman said would never be aired, and then I made sure that everyone in the room knew the consequences of repeating what was said. Ever. Anyone who defies that order will answer to me."

Oh my God. My mouth dropped open. I couldn't imagine what that asshole could've said that would make Lorne go so far as to have it stricken from existence. It seemed convenient that the footage on the news started with me blocking the councilman, not before.

Now I wasn't sure I wanted to know, but I absolutely needed to. I stared down at the floor to gather strength for knowing whatever would come next, and then I looked straight into Lorne's gaze. "Can you at least tell me what it was about?"

Lorne pressed his lips together and shook his head.

"Please."

Lorne's shoulders hunched and he looked so defeated, but he spoke anyway. "It was about you and Jason Murtagh and that day in the diner."

Oh.

My heart dropped, falling weightless to my feet, until it was smashed.

Oh.

Everyone in the ship was quiet, watching me, and I closed my eyes, shutting it out. Shutting out the memories and the horror and everything that haunted me. Everything that I'd already worked so hard to lock away today.

And then I realized something, and I turned, searching the room, until I saw him. "That's why you got so mad. In the gym. That's why you said…" I didn't need to finish it.

Eshrin pressed his fist to his heart. "I am sorry for what I said, and doubly sorry that I upset you." He bowed his head.

Oh.

I understood.

I understood why Lorne went to such lengths—and I appreciated it—but…

I squeezed my eyes tighter. "But you made it go away, and that makes it worse somehow. Like I'm trying to hide what happened, but I'm not. I'm not at all. I'm just trying to survive it and everything that happened after and before and I'm trying *so hard* to move on. I don't understand how anyone could throw that in my face—"

I felt Lorne's warmth as he wrapped his arms around me, pressing me so tight, too tight. Almost as if he thought he could staunch the wound in my soul if he held me tight enough.

And maybe he could. If anyone could, it was him.

After a moment, I took a breath, and said what was on my heart. "I'm not sure I'm fit to rule anyone, let alone the Aunare. Maybe the council is right. Maybe I'm too broken. Maybe I'm too hurt by SpaceTech to think rationally. And they're definitely right about speaking Aunare. I *can't*. I'll never be able to. That just isn't in the cards for me anymore."

Lorne stepped back just enough to grip my shoulders and force me to look at him. "The council is *wrong*." His words were angry. "You're not too broken. You've endured so much and you've kept on fighting. Everyone with half a brain and a soul in their body is so proud of you and your strength. There is no one more capable of saving the Aunare and winning this war against SpaceTech than you. I truly believe that you were born for this."

"I don't know. I don't know what I'm doing and—"

"And you're *learning*. This is all new for you, and to think that you'd get everything exactly right and that everything would go perfectly on your first day is insanity. You'll make mistakes, but to be perfectly clear—you didn't make one today. Don't let the council put those kinds of doubts in your mind. Remember that your station is above them. You don't need them to approve of you. They don't get to tell you who you are. Only you have that power. Don't you dare hand it over to that group of lazy, arrogant imbeciles."

I stared down at the floor and let his words sink in. Is that what I was doing? Did I let the High Council put doubts in my mind?

No. I didn't think so. They were already there.

I looked up at him again and hoped he'd understand. "I guess I don't really even know if I approve of me ruling. I think that's the problem. I'm doing it—" I said that part quickly so that he wouldn't freak out or cut me off. "—and I'll do my best, but I feel a little bit like a fraud. I want to go into the kitchens and get my own food, and apparently that's scandalous. And that's just a small thing. I saw the news and it makes sense that it was—"

"I thought I told you to stop watching it," he said it as if he were annoyed that I hadn't listened to him, but it wasn't that easy.

"I can't—" He started to talk, but I placed my hand over his lips so that he'd listen to me. "I can't stop watching the news. I have to know what they're saying so that I know what I'm up against. The only way I can strategize is by knowing. But honestly, it's not as bad as before…" I lowered my hand because I knew he was going to respond to what I said next. I didn't want to say it, but I felt like I had to put it out there. "I just don't think the Aunare want me as their queen, and if that's what everyone thinks, then maybe I shouldn't be."

"They don't know what they need. They don't know you, and they can't make that call. I do." He ran his fingers through my hair and then brushed a soft kiss against my lips. "You're going to be an amazing queen—I know it in my heart, in my soul, and I know it because I see your *fao'ana* and I have faith in them, in you, and in our culture to know that those *fao'ana* are true."

Maybe he had a point there.

"It's not just me wanting something from you. This is about you becoming who you truly were meant to be. If Liberation Week hadn't happened, no one would be questioning this. Not even a little bit. Not even you." He sighed. "But hiding on the estate hasn't been doing you any good. Not really. They used to know you, but they don't know you anymore. They've forgotten how excited they were when your *fao'ana* first appeared, and the Aunare were behind us getting married and being co-rulers when we were betrothed. They will be happy again."

"They were?" Because that seemed like the opposite of how they were now.

"They were overjoyed with us ruling together. *Everyone* agreed. This fear of you—this distrust of you becoming queen— is fear of the unknown in who you might have become. It's made worse by a fear of war and the danger that comes with being at war. So, tonight our job is to enjoy some time being us in front of our people. We're going to forget all the things that happened today and just have a nice, normal date where we talk about nice, normal things. I'd like to show them how you are when you're relaxed and having fun. They've seen angry Amihanna in the arena. They've seen you fighting for them—protecting them —in Ta'shena. Now, let them see *you*. The you that I know."

He was right. I never let anyone see me. That was the problem. Hiding who I was had become ingrained by necessity. On Earth, I needed to disappear into my hoodie and hope that it would keep anyone from looking too hard at me. Maybe that's why I'd never been on a date. Haden and I only hung out in places with the Crew or at his place. I never took him to the apartment I shared with my mom. The few times that Roan dragged me to Starlight, I kept the hoodie up. I never relaxed. Not even once.

Going from one extreme to another was unsettling. If that was the problem, I'd just have to try harder to relax. It would probably even be good for me.

The look on his face made me feel too exposed. There was a sadness in his eyes and some guilt that didn't belong there.

I'd lived. I was proud of that, even if I was still a little broken by my past. But I didn't regret the choices that I'd made or who I'd become because of my experiences.

I hadn't always liked myself, but I did now.

Whoever I was becoming—queen or not—was going to be a stronger, better version of myself.

Because I was a di Aetes.

I wouldn't give up. Not ever. I would fight. For my people. Earther and Aunare. Because I was both.

That was what I needed to remember. That was the kind of queen I wanted to become. The halfer High Queen.

That thought made me smile. It had a certain ring to it.

The halfer High Queen.

CHAPTER NINE

AMIHANNA

A FEW OF the guards went out to scope the market.

I hated this part. I hated that my guards were risking their lives for me, and I hated waiting here, doing nothing, while they searched for threats. I just wanted to get off this ship quickly before I chickened out. It wasn't like anyone knew we were coming to Ra'mi today, but the guards were doing their job to make sure we were safe.

A few more guards left the ship. And then a few more.

Ashino—Lorne's head guard—came back and motioned us forward. "The ship will stay here with a few guards. The rest of us will go with you. Your majesty, people saw me and the rest of the team, and they know what that means. Everyone moved to gather on the top floor of the market. If you want to wait a little bit, we can try to disperse the crowd. Or if you'd prefer—"

"That's all right, Ashino," Lorne said. "Do what you can to secure a path and I'll take care of the rest."

Ashino pressed his fist to his heart and bowed his head briefly. "Of course, your majesty. If you could give me a moment to start clearing the path before exiting the ship, that would be appreciated. I will do my best to have it ready when you come out." Ashino quickly pressed his fist to his heart again, and then rushed back down the ramp.

"Is this too much of a problem? Should we leave?" I really, really wanted to see Ra'mi in person and walk on those crazy light floors, but I didn't want to face a crowd, especially since I wasn't sure what they were going to do when they saw me. This could easily get very ugly, very quickly, but it seemed like I was the only one worried about it.

"It'll be okay," Lorne gripped my hand and tugged me down the ramp. "I promise. I've dealt with situations like this my whole life. You did, too. Before—" He gave me a tight smile and left off the obvious bit. Before I'd been stuck on Earth. Before I'd lost all my memories. Before everything had gone so horribly wrong. "It'll come back to you."

I wasn't sure about that. I still didn't like people watching me. I was doing better—much, much better—but I still had issues that came from hiding for so long.

And yet, I couldn't let something stupid like fear stop me. So, I gripped his hand a little tighter and kept pace with Lorne as we walked down the ramp. If he wasn't worried about this crowd turning into a mob, then I had to trust him.

We stepped onto the roof and our guards surrounded us. Some in front, some behind, and some covering left and right. There were too many people blocking the way for me to tell where the roof ended and the light platform began, but I could see a little beyond the guards to the crowd waiting for us.

Ashino wasn't joking. The people who had been milling about, buying food, hanging with their friends and family, had formed into a waiting wall. I couldn't even see the market behind them, and I wasn't convinced we could get through them. Ashino mentioned making a path, but there wasn't a path to be made.

I glanced behind me, and Eshrin was there. He raised a brow in question, as if to ask—did I want to go back?

It was his job to make sure I was comfortable in my

surroundings, not just for my safety, but also to help me main-
tain firm control of my power. We'd talked about my comfort
level around people so that he could help me stay comfortable.

I shook my head. *Not yet*, I mouthed to him. I was fine,
for now.

He pressed his fist to his heart, and I knew that if I changed
my mind, he'd get me back to the ship quickly.

Lorne gripped my hand, and I looked up at him.

"We can leave," he said the words, but the frown and the
small crease between his brows told me that he would be disappointed if we left.

"But you don't want to."

He shook his head. "It'll be better for us if we stay, but I
know this first time being out among our people won't be easy."

That was true for sure. I don't think he knew exactly why I
was afraid of the crowd, but it was better that he didn't. I wasn't
about to tell him how quickly a crowd could turn into a
murderous mob. I'd been there. I'd seen it. And I never, ever
wanted to be stuck hiding for my life again.

But knowing why I was afraid would only upset him more,
and he'd probably take me straight home. That was the worst
thing he could do for me right now. This fear of mobs was a
demon I needed to face, especially if this was what was standing
in the way of the Aunare accepting me as their queen. I'd made a
promise to Lorne to get the Aunare to accept me, and I wasn't
going to break it. Especially because of something as stupid as
fear.

As we got closer, the crowd stopped their chattering and
started humming.

I froze. The Aunare loved sound. They used it to heal their
minds and bodies, to change how they felt, and a bunch of other
things that seemed more fiction than reality. But it worked. That
was how I could explode things—melon, man, spaceship. It was
all because of the frequencies I could harness. That was my
power. My ability. That's what made me dangerous and why I

couldn't lose control. I could blow up this whole place if I got upset enough.

But their humming still felt a little weird to me. It wasn't as loud as an angry crowd would be, and I took that to be a good thing. What did it mean exactly?

We walked until there wasn't enough room for us to go any farther. The crowd kept up their humming, and my skin started to glow.

Ice it. I hated when it did that in public.

"What do we do now?" I said in Lorne's ear.

"We'll say something, and then we'll have our date."

The guards shifted so that he could step in front of them, and he started to move forward, closer to the crowd.

I gripped his arm, stopping him.

Was he crazy? He couldn't walk into the crowd. Anyone could be in there. Someone could hurt—

He looked back at me. "I'll be fine. Promise." He brushed a quick kiss on my cheek, and then he turned to the crowd and held up his hand.

The humming stopped freakily fast.

Lorne spoke in clear Aunare, and the gathered crowd laughed.

Damn it. What was he saying?

I patted my pockets, but no translator. I closed my eyes and tried to remember where I'd left it.

By the bathroom sink. *Idiot.* I'd forgotten it in the dish beside the bathroom sink for the meeting and then didn't think about it again.

Oh well. Too late now.

A voice cleared behind me.

Eshrin held out his hand, but his eyes never stopped scanning the crowd. He kept holding out his hand, until I looked at it. On his palm was a tiny device.

My translator.

Eshrin really needed a raise. He was doing a great job.

"Thank you. You're amazing." I snatched the translator from his hand and popped the device into my ear. I pressed my fingertip against it for three seconds, and the little *ding-dong-dang* sounded.

The device was controlled by my line of sight and would pick up anything anyone was saying. So far, distance hadn't been an issue.

As the translator activated, the sound around me muffled in that ear, the signal that it was going to start actively translating.

I stared at some of the onlookers.

"She looks so regal next to the king."

"I don't know how someone so small could do what she did. Protecting the city like that?"

That didn't sound bad. Was showing up somewhere all I needed to do to get their approval? If so, then maybe just doing the interview and answering Himani's questions would be enough to win over everyone else?

"She doesn't seem like a queen."

"What is she wearing?"

Ugh. Really? This was why I hated translators.

And damn it. I'd gone for the nicer pants and a silky tank-blouse that Almya insisted on instead of the leggings and loose sweater that I'd wanted to wear after my workout. Now I wished I'd gone with what I wanted because apparently no matter what I wore, it would be the wrong thing. I couldn't please everyone and trying would only make me hate them all.

I'd promised Lorne that I would win over everyone, and for a second, I'd thought maybe it wasn't going to be that hard. But it was and I had no idea how to keep from breaking my promise.

Lorne started speaking again, and I aimed my gaze at him. The translation kicked in a fraction of a second later.

"—are here to have a bit of an evening away from our duties. I know that you have questions and concerns about what might be coming in terms of SpaceTech, but from one person to another, I would ask you to please let us have a normal night out. Amihanna hasn't

gotten to enjoy Ta'shena, and that's a shame. Ra'mi is one of my favorite spots, and I'm quite excited to show it to her." He looked back at me and winked. *"I think I can even get her to taste the* a'mian."

The people laughed, and I knew I'd missed a joke. I didn't know what *a'mian* was, but the translator didn't have a word in English to translate it into. From the smirk on Lorne's face, I was pretty sure I didn't want to find out what *a'mian* was. It was going to be gross for sure.

God. He was as bad as the kitchen staff.

"We'll stand here for a moment while you take pictures, and then I would truly appreciate the chance to share one of my favorite spots with my mirror soul, as any of you would do on one of your dates."

Mirror soul.

Shalshasa.

That's one word I didn't need translated. That's what we were.

I still didn't fully understand it, but I knew that I felt better when Lorne was around. I needed him more and more every day, and it was almost as if he'd woven himself through my soul.

Lorne motioned me forward to stand beside him in front of the guards. It took me a second to start moving, but as soon as I got close enough, he tucked me into his side. We stood there, posing like that together, while the people got their pictures. I was pretty sure the pained smile I'd pasted on my face was going to make the pictures turn out a special kind of awful, but it was the best I could do.

After a moment, he turned to his guard, and as they stepped forward, the crowd actually parted to make room. I'd been so sure that they wouldn't let us through, but they did without the guards needing to step in and make them. Which showed how much the people respected Lorne. They wanted him to have a night off.

It was surprising to me, but I wasn't sure why. It's not like I had any experience with being in public on Sel'Ani before. If

SpaceTech's leaders were out and about, I wasn't sure I would've recognized them—clearly I hadn't recognized Jason Murtaugh when he walked into the diner—but I was usually too busy trying to avoid them to even look closely at their faces. I couldn't imagine a mob like this around Earth's leaders without it turning dangerous.

But this was different. This was Sel'Ani. And Lorne was the High King.

We grew closer to the market entrance, and Lorne stepped onto the light floor. He tugged me forward, but I couldn't seem to move. All I could do was stare at the floor.

The light was like a very translucent misty color and completely transparent. Even knowing that people were on it and completely safe, it was hard to take that first step onto the path. I had to do it, but it seemed like I'd fall to my death if I tried to walk on it.

And yet, I knew I had to do it anyway.

I swallowed down the fear. I'd done so many worse things. At least this wasn't lava and I wasn't in a suit and my lungs weren't going to burn from the heat in the air.

I could do this.

I heard a far off laugh, and I looked down to the next level. Two children were playing a game of chase around some tables.

I was being ridiculous. If this was safe enough for children to play on, then I really, seriously could do this.

I took a step.

My stomach dropped to my feet. I knew I wouldn't fall down a thousand feet to my death, but I couldn't make my brain believe that. I must've made a sound as I moved because I heard some laughing from around me.

I was being stupid—maybe—but it didn't look like anything was there to catch my fall except a beam of light. Which wouldn't do anything to stop a death plummet.

Except the light had a spongy texture.

I stared down at the faintly tinted blue light. Completely flipping out on how frosty it was. I bounced a few times and turned to Lorne. "What is it?"

He leaned down close to me. "Magic," he whispered in my ear.

A surprised laugh slipped free. "Shut up." I shoved him, but he didn't really move. "What is it?"

He was grinning at me when he stepped back. "Honestly, it might as well be magic. I don't understand how it works. That's for the architecture and physics Aunare bloodlines, but as far as I know, this is the only structure of its kind."

"It's honestly amazing." I took another step, and then another.

Instead of crowding around our wall of guards, the people who had been watching us started to disperse slowly back into the market. The noise around me grew louder as people picked up their conversations, heading to different vendors selling wares and food, and playing with their friends and family.

I expected most of them to follow us, but it was as if their fascination with us was suddenly over.

"They're not going to follow us?" I asked Lorne.

He looked down at me as we walked holding hands. "I know that you have a lot of mistrust with the Aunare, but we aren't horrible. By speaking to them and letting them know what we were doing here, I satisfied their curiosity. I let them take their pictures so that they can have memories of us being here, which earned us some space. They won't follow us to take our pictures. At least the majority of them won't. They have their own lives and plans for the night."

"Even with both of us here?" Lorne had been here before, so maybe he was old news. But I hadn't been to Ra'mi before. "I know I'm a bit of an unknown, and not exactly liked."

"Honestly, I was worried that it might go differently tonight, and to some extent that's true. It is going a little differently."

Lorne motioned around us, and I took a second look. People

were moving on, but they were also sneaking looks at us. "Normally they wouldn't be doing that," he said.

Okay. It was just my own experience with mobs that tainted what I expected, and I was happy to be wrong. "Everyone is watching, but they'll give us space to have a date." I wanted confirmation that I was understanding correctly.

"Exactly. Which is what I'd hoped for."

I wasn't sure what I expected, but not this. "I'm not really used to being out in public, but I don't really feel unsafe. It's weird." I didn't even really mind that people were watching.

"That's a good thing—a really good thing—because you are safe."

"Yeah." But it was still weird for me.

I kept scanning the crowd, but my translator was kicking in and out. It was more than a little disorienting, not to mention annoying. I took the device out and tucked it away in my pocket as we moved to a set of light stairs and down to the next level.

Smells drifted up to us, and my stomach grumbled.

Lorne tugged me faster. "Come on. I can't stand the sound of your hunger. We need to fix that first. There's a food stall just down this way that's my favorite. The chef's cooking isn't quite as good as Nori's, but there are a few treats that I think you'll enjoy."

"No tricks, though. No way am I trying the *a'mian*, whatever that is."

Lorne laughed, and a little kid darted up to us, waved, and then darted back to his mother, who was looking embarrassed. Her skin was glowing slightly as she whispered in sharp Aunare to the boy.

I waved at them as we kept walking, and she bowed her head saying something I couldn't understand.

"She's apologizing," Lorne said to me before nodding to the mother.

I didn't like that. He hadn't done anything wrong. "Tell her not to be too upset with him. Bravery is something to be admired, and I actually like kids." A child's innocence didn't last long on Earth, but whenever I saw it, I equally envied it and wanted to protect it—and them—fiercely.

Lorne grinned as if I'd done something to make him proud, which was dumb. I hadn't done anything, and his look made me uncomfortable. He spoke quickly to the mom, and then we started moving again. I busied myself with staring at all of the stalls we were passing.

The food stalls circled this level of the market. Hundreds of short tables with benches on either side took up the center of the floor. We walked past so many of them, and at more than a few, the food they were serving looked good and smelled even better. I wasn't sure where he was leading me, but I was going to give him a few minutes.

Except I was starving. So maybe it'd be only one minute.

I opened my mouth to tell Lorne to quit dragging me around and get me some food already, but he stopped walking. I stared at the stall with a line that was nearly twenty people deep, easily the longest line so far. We were so far from the stall that I couldn't even see what they were serving. There was a bright red awning over the stall with swirling dark blue Aunare script across it. The menu off to the side didn't even have pictures, which meant it was no help.

His spot was definitely the most popular, which meant it had to be the best, but I was starving.

My stomach growled again, and I pressed my fist against it to make the ache stop. "This line will take forever. Can't we go to one of the other stalls? Say one without a million people in line? Like one of the thirty million other stalls we passed?"

"Wait over there." Lorne motioned to one of the empty tables. "And try to be patient."

"You were the one who took away my bag of *ba'na* on the trip over here," I muttered mostly to myself because Lorne and Ashino were already striding to the front of the line.

Someone moved up beside me, and I glanced over to see Eshrin. "He's going to cut?"

I'd never cut a line in my life. It just felt so wrong to put myself in front of so many people that had been obviously waiting for longer than I had. I'd been in lines that wrapped around buildings and went for blocks hoping that by the time I got to the front, they'd have food or shelter or something left for me and my mom.

They usually didn't, and sometimes we went hungry and slept outside, but I never cut. Not ever.

"Should I yell at him to come back? I can wait. Really."

Eshrin shrugged. "He's the High King. He doesn't have to wait, especially if you're hungry."

Sure, he was High King, but that shouldn't mean that he got to cut. "He doesn't need to do that. I'm hungry, but honestly, I've been much hungrier before. On Earth, I went days without food and..." I slowly stopped talking when Eshrin's skin flashed brighter.

Whoops.

Now I'd made it awkward, and I was pretty sure if I went after Lorne to tell him not to cut, I'd be starting something I didn't want to.

"He's our *king*." Eshrin's words were tight and angry, and I was pretty sure it didn't have anything to do with Lorne. "No one will mind. In fact, if he didn't, people would be upset."

Upset? That sounded a little over the top to me. "Why?"

"Because it's an honor to be able to help the High King when he spends his days making sure that all of us are safe. It's not every day that a normal person gets to do something for the High King. Waiting a minute longer isn't a huge burden for them, especially when it's a way for them to show their thanks. No one will be angry that he went to the front. So relax. He'll be back in a moment."

"Okay," I said softly.

I really was hungry. The *ba'na* was high in calories due to the sugar, but that meant that it burned off quickly.

Lorne moved through the crowd at the stall, and I kept expecting people to get mad that he was cutting. But as soon as people saw him, they moved out of his way. No one seemed to be annoyed or put out by it.

Fine. If it was only me with the problem, then I would have to let it go.

While I stood beside the tables, I looked around the market— scanning for anyone that could be a threat and tried to be patient as my stomach slowly ate itself, but then my eye caught on a vid screen across the way from me. My fingers touched the translator in my pocket before I had a second to think about it, but I stopped myself before pulling it out.

This was our night off, but I couldn't look away.

Footage of Earth filled the screens. The vids from Earth got smaller to make room for two Aunare women arguing. Something must've happened with SpaceTech, and I knew it was probably a good thing that I'd left the translator in my pocket. Time seemed to slow as I watched the screen move to images of Earther streets. I wasn't sure what city that was, but it wasn't Albuquerque.

There was a fight on the street, and suddenly, I felt homesick.

It was insane. I shouldn't feel homesick. Especially not when there was violence and unrest there. Earth was beyond dangerous for me—especially now that everyone knew what I looked like and who I was—but it was home. If something was happening there, it felt like I should be there to do something.

Maybe I needed to reach out to the Crew again. Roan hadn't heard back yet, but maybe if I tried something else, some other channel, another board, something. I just wanted to know that they were okay.

"What's wrong?" Lorne asked as he walked up to us.

"Nothing." And there really was nothing wrong. Or there shouldn't have been. I was safe and so far away from whatever was going on back home, but when I looked at the screen again, it felt like I was ignoring something.

It was stupid. I knew it was stupid, and so I pushed it away. "Nothing's wrong." This time I said it with confidence. "I'm good." Because I was here with Lorne, on a date, waiting for food, having a nice night in the most amazing place. How could I be anything other than happy?

A man in an apron approached us with a basket of food that smelled amazing. He said something to Lorne and handed the basket over with his arms extended and head bowed.

Lorne took it and said something softly back with a smile. Knowing Lorne, he was giving some kind of compliment. I didn't have to understand his words to know that.

And I guessed that meant it was my turn to look at *him* with pride.

I knew all too well what bad rulers looked like, and Lorne was nothing of the sort. Even if he had cut the line, he was a fantastic king. A king of the people. A king that his people would love, not fear. Seeing him out in public only drove that fact home a little more.

I was in awe of him and the ease that he had as he chatted softly with the chef while everyone looked on. I'd never felt that comfortable. It wasn't my fault. If things had been different, I might have the same ease as he did, but then I wouldn't be who I was today.

I was proud of who I'd become in order to survive, but that didn't mean I couldn't wish to grow into something better. Lorne made me want that for myself. To be better.

The chef pressed a fist to his heart, and then rushed back to his stall, with all the waiting hungry people.

Lorne motioned to the tables with the baskets in his hands. "Let's find a place to sit and eat."

"Finally." I hoped more food was coming because one basket of food wasn't going to be enough. Especially if he wanted any of it.

The guards moved quickly—some forming a loose wall around us as we chose a table, while the rest stood back a little—patrolling the area and protecting our exits.

I usually didn't love having so many guards, but I had to admit that having them there made me able to let go just a little bit. Just enough to meet Lorne's eyes and focus on our date.

I sat on one of the benches, and Lorne sat across from me, patiently watching me, waiting for me to relax.

"Okay?" He asked after a moment.

I nodded slowly as I looked around the market. People were still watching us and we still had guards around us, but suddenly none of that mattered. It was just me and Lorne and most importantly, whatever was in the basket.

I stuck a finger along one edge, tipping the basket my way to peek inside. There were diced cubes of what I thought had to be meat, but I couldn't assume that it was. Not on Sel'Ani. Not so far away from anything that I knew.

The maybe-meat was served over a bed of little golden bits of something that looked fried and crunchy. There was a tiny bowl of something yellow with blue flecks in it that had to be a sauce for dipping, but again—assuming anything could be a minefield of mistakes. Whatever this was could be savory or sweet or completely disgusting.

"Okay. I have no idea what it is. Explain." I pointed a finger at him. "And no tricks. I'm way too hungry for worms or any other shenanigans."

"Worms?"

"*Nic'natarani.*"

"What?" he said with a startled laugh. "Who gave you that?"

"Someone in the kitchens." I stared suspiciously at the baskets. "And my father let me eat it."

Lorne laugh started off small. "I can't believe you ate it."

"Well, to be fair, I didn't technically eat it. I spit it out." I leaned across the table to whisper at him. "The worm was still wiggling."

Lorne's laughter got bigger, louder, and now people were staring.

"Okay. It's not that funny."

"No. No, it really is that funny. *Nic'natarani* is revolting." He stuck out his tongue just a little. "I can't believe Rysden didn't stop you. I can't believe I missed it."

I gave him a look that told him he was asking for trouble.

He held up his hands. "No tricks. Not when you're so hungry that I can hear your stomach." He stared into the basket. "I guess the most similar I had on Earth was a beef kabob. Sort of. This meat is different—fattier and more tender. It's a small animal called *yhano* that lives along the beaches, but it's not seafood. It's seafood adjacent. There isn't a thing like it on Earth, so you're just going to have to trust me that it is delicious." He picked up one of the crispy golden pieces. "And these fried bits are a veggie called *kiom* that you'll like. It's like micro squash that's tossed in some bread bits and fried. It's good. Crispy on the outside, soft and mushy on the inside." He dropped the *kiom* back inside the basket and pushed it toward me. "Try it."

I wanted to, but I was a little nervous. I could feel everyone watching me, but I knew that no one could really get a good view of me around the guards. If I hated it, hopefully no one would notice, but I didn't want to offend.

Screw it. It smelled good.

I held my hand out, and Lorne passed me a fork. I stabbed one tiny cube of meat. As soon as it hit my tongue, I closed my eyes and moaned. It was spicy and tangy and the meat was so tender that it nearly melted in my mouth. I was hungrier than I'd thought and this was really hitting the spot.

When I opened my eyes, Lorne was grinning at me. "Dip the next bite in this." He tapped the cup of sauce. "It's a creamy, tangy dip. No tricks, even if it would look awful to an Earther."

"If it's gross, I know where you sleep. I can—"

"I never knew a little sauce could turn you into a coward."

I narrowed my gaze at him. "I never knew you were a jerk."

Lorne leaned back as he laughed deep and loud. The sound warmed my soul, and I stabbed another bit of the meat and dipped it.

I took another bite.

The creamy dip cooled some of the heat that was burning my mouth. It was so good, I couldn't help but want more. I slid the basket closer to me. "This is mine. Where's yours?"

Lorne just grinned at me. "More is coming. He rushed out a basket for you, but I ordered a lot." He tapped the basket. "You eat up."

Someone spoke behind Eshrin and he turned, talking to a woman, who handed him some drinks. He set them on the table between us, and that seemed to set off some agreement that we were open for food.

For a while, Lorne and I just ate. Not talking about anything of substance, except about what was in the plates and containers and baskets. Chefs from all the stalls kept bringing food, and we kept eating. Until I wasn't sure where I would put any more.

And then I sat there with my elbows on the table, leaning toward Lorne and thankful to be here, at this market, having a date. It almost felt like everything could be normal for a second.

I could have a million easy nights like this with him, and it wouldn't be enough.

It could never be enough.

And so I would talk to him now and make tonight count in every way that I could. Because I knew that everything always changed.

Everything would change when all I wanted was to hang on to this and stay here, but wishing for that was like trying to hold a shooting star in my hands.

Impossible.

But boy, did I want the impossible with him. I wanted it more than I wanted air.

CHAPTER TEN

LORNE

THE BUSY RA'MI market faded from my awareness, and I was grateful that I was sitting across the table from Amihanna, watching her relax. More and more vendors brought their offerings to us, and it was rude to turn them down. Which meant we'd both eaten too much food. Still, it was nice to make Amihanna try new things.

A few chefs brought things to us I knew she wouldn't like— Aunare delicacies that I didn't even like—and I let her try them just to keep her on her toes. Although nothing as bad as *nic'-natarani*. It was a game we used to play. One that clearly Rysden remembered, with good reason. We'd embarrassed him more than a few times at important dinners, but to be fair, important usually meant boring. If no one entertained us, Amihanna and I often found ways to entertain ourselves, which tended to end with us in trouble.

But playing the game today meant I had to try to eat some of the ones I didn't care for when normally I'd just move the food around in the basket a little to make it look like I'd eaten enough not to insult the chef. Teasing her was too much fun, especially today when she was trying to pretend that she liked everything she tried. But it was so plain to see what she didn't enjoy.

Somewhere along the way, Amihanna's shoulders had lost their stiffness, she smiled more, and leaned toward me as she spoke. Having a normal night together filled my heart with the peace and contentment that I had been missing for thirteen years. And even though we were playing the same game as we used to and having fun, it wasn't even the same as when we were younger.

Tonight was infinitely better.

Even as I was feeling that peace of being with her, I knew it was temporary. It was like paper-thin crystal. One hard breath and it would shatter.

The people needed to accept Amihanna. I knew she wanted to try to make that happen, but I wasn't sure it was possible. I needed her to be ready to argue with the allies, but she wasn't. She was still getting used to everything here, and I knew she needed time. For everything.

I knew Fynea, Lorne's good friend and head assistant, and Roan were busy trying to arrange the interview with Himani, but it was taking too long. That's why we were here. I always wanted time with her, but I also wanted to get her out there in front of the people. I wanted them to love Amihanna as much as I did, and even as I thought that, an image on the vid screen across the way caught my eye.

They'd moved on from the report about SpaceTech to Amihanna. Her face on the screen was what caught my attention. I was too far from the screen to hear what they were saying, but I could read the flowing gold script.

Goddess take it. I freed the media. I let them be honest, and I thought that meant that they'd report about her truthfully.

But now they were saying she was too busy having fun with me to rule. That she'd failed in her first High Council meeting, and that now she was out with me at the market instead of figuring out how to fix her mistakes.

They had no idea what they were speaking about. No idea. Had they forgotten that the High Council actually held no power? If she never showed her face to them again, it wouldn't matter. But she had to because she could hone her skills to rule with them. She could make mistakes with them. Mistakes she couldn't afford with our allies.

"What are you thinking?" Amihanna's question snapped me back into the present.

"Hmm?"

Amihanna waved a fork in my direction. "I can feel you getting angrier and more worried by the second. If you don't cut it out, you're going to be glowing brighter than the floor in this place in about ten and three-quarter seconds."

I couldn't tell her the truth—that the news was lying about her again. I wasn't ruining this evening by talking about the things we were both already worried about. I wanted a break from all of that, and I knew she wanted one, too. So, I brushed the fear and anger and worry away until I was sure she couldn't sense it anymore. And then I shoved it a little farther.

She took another bite and chewed slowly. "Avoidance," she said finally. "I like that. Not healthy, and I'm pretty sure you wouldn't let me get away with it, but I get it. I'll allow it."

She'd allow it? I wanted to laugh, but then she might try to get me to change my mind. I wasn't going to budge on this. Not tonight. Tonight, we were getting that break.

I leaned forward, resting my forearms on the table. "So, what do you think?"

"Of?"

I straightened. "This." I motioned around us.

She tilted back a little so that she could see the floor and the lower levels of the market through the light. "I think that it's a very good thing Roan isn't here tonight. He would absolutely hate this market."

"Really?" The market was amazing. I honestly couldn't think of any reason why he'd hate it, and I thought I knew Roan pretty well. Food, drinks, plenty of women to flirt with. What more could he want? "Why exactly would he hate it?" I wasn't insulted. Just curious.

She sat straight again. "To be fair, most humans would hate this place. A lot of them have this thing with heights." She took a sip of water.

Oh. Right. I'd forgotten. Declan—the man I called my Earther brother—used to be afraid, but we'd grown up together since our tenth year. Due to a ridiculous treaty our fathers made, we split our time on Earth for six-months, followed by six-months on Sel'Ani. Declan had been keeping up with me for so long that he'd pretty much conquered his fear of heights.

"Heights don't bother you?" I asked her. Sometimes I wondered how many Aunare tendencies she'd lost with her memories.

She made a face like I'd said something absurd. "No. Otherwise, I probably wouldn't be so obsessed with the climbing wall."

Right. That made me feel better. I would've hated it if she'd been afraid this whole time. I felt like I would've known if she had been, but I needed to know for sure.

"But yeah, I don't mind heights, and I seriously love this place. Although, it *is* kind of crazy how you can see all the way down to the ground."

"There's definitely nothing else quite like it, but I'm extremely biased. This is a market in my capital city."

"Right." Amihanna pushed the baskets down the table. "Well, I'm full. And if I sit here any longer, I'm going to barf. I can't look at any more food, let alone eat it. So, what's next?"

There was so much to show her that I wasn't sure where to start. "This is the food level, clearly. The rest have some specialty foods but mostly for eating later. Pantry items and such. Other than that, there's clothes, household items, and tech mixed together. This dining plaza is the only level that's just one thing."

"So we wander?"

"Unless there's something you wanted in particular? I know

it pretty well. I'm sure I can find you anything you're looking for."

She thought for a second. "No. I'm not really looking for anything. I mean, I have more right now than I've ever had before. What more could I possibly need?"

She hadn't meant to cut me with that, but it stung all the same. I wanted to forget what she'd been through the last thirteen years, but I couldn't. I'd never forget. And yet, it still snuck up on me sometimes.

What she had now was more than she'd ever had before? I knew she wouldn't have said it if it weren't true, but it was upsetting and unsettling and made my heart ache for her. She didn't have anything besides clothes, a tablet, and her go-bags stashed around the estate. That wasn't a lot of things. She could have so much more. She could have anything she wanted.

I wanted to press her for more information. I needed to know more.

What was it really like there on Earth?

How did she get through Liberation Week?

Where did she go? Where did she work? Did she go to school? What happened if she got sick? Where did she live before she was arrested? I knew it was an apartment in Albuquerque, but I didn't know what it was like. Did she have enough clothes? Food? A bed to sleep in?

I wasn't a complete idiot. I knew wherever she lived, it probably wasn't nice, but it was hard for me to picture her life on Earth. I didn't know much about those thirteen years other than it was hard. I knew bits and pieces from her nightmares—things she screamed in her sleep or explanations about what she'd been dreaming about—but it wasn't enough to make out a whole picture.

I shoved all of those questions burning inside of me far, far away. I knew eventually I would cave and ask for more details, but not tonight. Not when it might upset her. Not when she might have nightmares or flashbacks because I'd been stupid enough to ask for more than she was ready to give.

Amihanna was in a good spot right now, and I wouldn't let my thirst to know everything hurt her.

So, instead, I asked her something else. "Would you like to explore the other levels of the market?"

"Yeah. Actually, that sounds pretty nice," she said, not noticing that I was still barely breathing through the searing, stabbing pain her words had left inside my soul.

I cleared my throat. "We can wander." I walked around the table, and reached a hand out. She took it, and the burn started to ease a little.

But only because I vowed to myself that if she saw something she liked, we were buying it. No arguing allowed.

Amihanna stood still, glancing around the market nervously, and tried to pull her hand free.

"What is it? Do you see something?"

She was very good at spotting undercover SpaceTech operatives. She'd found some from footage of this market in particular, and I wasn't sure I'd ever feel completely at ease here again.

I glanced around, trying to see what was worrying her, but I'd bet my life that aside from a few easily spotted foreigners, everyone here was Aunare.

"Don't you need to pay all these people?"

Oh. Well, damn. That wasn't what I was expecting. I gripped her hand tighter. "I love that you're worried about them."

"Well, the food cost them money to get, and then time to prepare it. The basket. The cup. The fork. It all cost them something, and—"

I grinned at her.

"What? This isn't funny." She tried to shove me, but it was a pitiful move. "I'm being serious right now."

"I know." And I loved that. I tried to get rid of my grin and failed. "I know you're serious and that this is a serious topic. I don't take money around Sel'Ani because everyone knows who I am. They know to send a payment request to Fynea—who tracks where I go—and she immediately sends payment, usually more than requested, unless they ask for the cost of goods to be taken from their taxes. In which case, we honor their request and a note is made on their accounts. That's why everyone was rushing to bring us more and more food."

"Oh." She looked almost disappointed. "I thought they were doing it because you were their king."

"Sure. That, too. But they'll be reimbursed and then some. Does that take away any guilt you're feeling now?"

She let out a breath. "Yes. It really does." The tension that had come on so suddenly faded away, and she finally stepped away from the table. "Where to next?"

"One of the lower floors? We could work our way back up to the ship, and see if anything catches your eye along the way."

"Sure."

As we walked, the guards moved to keep us covered. I'd always felt safe in Ta'shena, and I wasn't going to let one attack keep me from doing what I wanted in my own city. I usually wouldn't have brought so many guards—usually just Ashino and one or two others—but now I was High King. More importantly, at least in my mind, Amihanna was with me.

I wasn't risking her again. SpaceTech had gotten too close to taking her away from me *again*, and I wasn't going to give them another chance.

There was no way I'd ever tell her that. There was no reason for me to intentionally make her that annoyed with me.

I know what she'd say. That she could defend herself and had done so for a long time without me. That we'd found so many hidden operatives and she would spot any others before I could. But that still left too much room for disaster.

I didn't know if we'd found all of SpaceTech's operatives on Sel'Ani. There was no way we could ever really know if we got them all. Not until it was too late. So, I assumed that there were a lot more just waiting for their shot to take her down. Because the

reality was that there were very likely more in Ta'shena. Probably more here in this very market. Maybe even in this market
watching us right now.

A tiny thread of fear started to weave its way through my
soul and I cut it before Amihanna could sense anything. And
still, I kept my eyes open, searching for the tells that Amihanna
had taught me.

"Are you okay?" she asked again.

"Yes."

She glanced at the vid screens quickly, and then went back to
it and stared. "Oh. I bet they're saying awful things about me.
That's why you're upset?"

"Yes." That was part of the reason anyway.

"I'm probably causing all kinds of problems for you."

"No." No, she wasn't. She wasn't a problem. Amihanna was
a gift.

"I know that they hate me. Or at least they don't like me
much or trust me or believe that I should rule with you. I'm not
sure how to change that. I know I made a promise—"

"Amihanna. It's not you alone that has to change their
perception of you. It's—"

"No. I'm going to figure it out." She had that impossibly
stubborn tone now, and I knew it'd do no good to argue with
her. "I know there's a solution. I'm just not sure what."

This was something I'd let her take responsibility for because
she wanted it. Not because of a promise or that I even needed
that from her, but because she'd wanted to do something as a
ruler. It was the first time she'd wanted to take part, and I don't
think she even realized it.

So, I was letting her go with it, but I wasn't sure if this was
something that could be easily accomplished. It certainly wasn't
going to happen overnight. I hoped she wouldn't stress or get
frustrated, but I'd watch her and help as much as she'd let me.

For now, she needed a distraction. This was a date, and she
was going to have fun. It was my mission.

I tugged on her hand, pulling her away from the vid screens. "Tonight might help, but I think they just need to get used to seeing you—to seeing *us*. They need to see you as a queen, to understand you, to get to know you. They don't understand who you are, and you're such an unknown. No one knows anything about you or what you experienced or how you lived while you were on Earth. And since they don't know that, they can't understand who you are now. Unknowns can be scary. So, I think that's mostly what this is."

I saw a look cross her face for a second before she shut it down, and I wasn't sure what it meant.

"What is it?"

She blinked a few times and I knew she was about to lie. It's what she did when she was little, but she never lied to me. It was always a look she gave her parents.

It was in that moment that I knew she was hiding something from me. I wanted to call her on it, but I was keeping something from her, too. So, it felt like I shouldn't push, unless I was going to tell her the truth about what was happening with our allies.

And I couldn't do that. She'd already been adjusting too much. It wasn't fair to pile something else on top.

So, I kept my questions to myself again and led her through the market.

Tonight would be nice. We would have fun, and I was going to forget about the media and just enjoy her company because I never thought I'd ever get the chance to see her again, let alone be lucky enough have a real date with her. If they couldn't see what an amazing ruler she'd be—if she hadn't proven it yet—I wasn't sure how to make them see.

I needed to be patient. I would work on that, but it was hard when I wanted so much.

I wanted the Aunare to accept her as their ruler.

I wanted our allies to join our side against SpaceTech.

I wanted her to already be my wife and queen, but that

wouldn't happen for a little bit. The people needed time, and if I was being honest, so did Amihanna.

And for Amihanna, I would do anything. I could wait forever for her.

She was here, by my side, walking with me through one of my favorite places on my home planet, and that was enough.

By the Goddess, that was more than enough.

CHAPTER ELEVEN

AMIHANNA

THE DEEPER WE got into the shopping section of Ra'mi market, the more tense I became. There was too much to see, too much to look at, and Lorne kept offering up stuff for me to buy—a painting, a decorative bowl, the blanket was nice, but why did I need any of this stuff?

Why was he so insistent?

Why did he think I needed anything more?

Why didn't he understand that I had more than enough? I had food. I had clothes. I had a safe place to sleep—granted, there'd been some trouble with that, but I had guards to help me feel safer wherever I went. I even had go-bags with money and passports and food and everything I could ever want in them.

I had enough. I had more than enough. I didn't need to buy anything.

I didn't *want* to buy anything.

My temper was starting to fray, and I didn't want that either. Losing my shit in public would be so much worse than losing it in the privacy of my gym. But I didn't want to explain why I was uncomfortable either. Both would ruin our night. This was our date. Our *first* date. I wanted it to be perfect.

And yet, by staying silent, I was already ruining it.

I couldn't win, and that meant the only thing I could do was fail. And it was so iced. I felt so unbelievably iced.

We passed by a stall, and Lorne paused, talking to the owner. I glanced at what was on the table.

Earrings. I touched my earlobes. I didn't wear earrings. I didn't have them pierced, and I'd never even thought about it. The only jewelry I wore was my engagement ring, and I never really owned anything else. I didn't have the money for it before, and now...

And now I didn't see the point of it. The engagement ring stood for something. It was meaningful and I loved it. But the rest were pretty but pointless.

Lorne turned to me, and pointed to a pair. "Do you like them?" He gave me a hopeful look, but I didn't get it.

I shrugged. "They're pretty." I guessed. If you wanted a pair, they were small enough. Just little glints of a blue glittering stone that would sparkle in the light.

"Do you want them?"

Me? "No." I didn't need anything that fancy. "I'm good."

Lorne shoved his hands into his pockets and let out a sigh. He looked so defeated as he said something quickly to the man at the stall and then started walking away.

Okay. I was going to have to say something. I had to lay it out there, and he'd just have to understand.

I took a few quick steps to catch up with him. "I'm sorry." I figured that was the best way to start.

"There's no sorry." He tugged his hands through his hair, and I knew there was so much more he wasn't saying. The man was frustrated.

I was frustrating him.

I waited for him to finish explaining, and ended up poking him in the side when he didn't.

He gave me a smile that was mostly sad. "You didn't want

the earrings, but... I want to buy you something. Anything." His fingers raked through his hair again. "Please, pick something out. Let me buy you something."

Oh boy. The guy was really miserable. I took a quick glance around the market but it was too much. There were so many stalls and so much noise and people and I had no idea what to tell him to buy for me. Nothing seemed important enough that I should waste good money on it, and yet, I kept searching the stalls, hoping I could honestly point to something and say *yes, please, buy me that. I need that.*

"It can be something small." His voice was so soft and pleading that it made my heart ache. "It could be something that would help you remember our first date."

I tucked a piece of his hair behind his ear. "I'm not going to forget this. It's not possible. I don't need anything to help me remember it."

He tilted his head at me, as if trying to tell if I was lying.

Did he really think that was possible? Did he think I wasn't having fun if I wasn't buying anything? "I'm having a really good time. I promise. I just haven't seen anything that I need yet." If I did, I'd buy it. Probably. If it wasn't too expensive. We'd probably already spent a fortune on food, but I wasn't going to tell him that. No way.

He started walking again, and I kept pace beside him. "Are you having a good time?"

"I am. I mean, I was. Until now." Man, if Roan were here, he'd make a joke to somehow explain to Lorne why I wasn't a big shopper, but I didn't have that ability to make everything funny. Especially things that were decidedly unfunny.

Lorne grabbed my hand and stopped walking again.

I looked up at him, but I couldn't find any words. I didn't know how to tell him the truth without hurting him, and that just plain sucked.

"Just tell me. I can feel you wrestling with something inside you, and it's making me more tense. So, just tell me. Do you want to go home?"

"No," I said quickly. "No. I don't want to go home. Not like this. I don't want to fight."

"I'm not fighting. I just want to make you happy."

"I am happy." I needed to say it. To be honest about how I felt. To stop being a chicken and put it out there and then deal with whatever came next. "Please don't be angry."

"I'm not angry."

"Yes, you might get angry..." But I was going to say it anyway. "I just don't feel comfortable spending money, especially when I don't feel like it's mine—"

Lorne's glow lit up the market, and everything grew quiet. I could sense our guards moving to surround us, but I didn't dare look away from Lorne.

Instead, I kept stumbling through my explanation. "—and I don't really need anything. I mean, why do people even wear earrings?"

"Because they're pretty." Now he sounded outright frustrated, like he was trying to negotiate with a crazy person, but we just weren't seeing things the same way.

I needed him to understand where I was coming from, which meant I was going to have to explain more than I wanted to. *Oh man.* This was going to hurt him and I hated that, but there was no more avoiding it.

"That's the thing. I just—I'm too practical. I never bought things because they were pretty. We didn't have money for that. We barely had money for food, and for chunks of time, we sometimes didn't have money to have a place to sleep. It's so hard for me to go from being so poor, so hungry, and barely surviving, to you trying to buy everything you see for me." I reached out to him, but his hands were still shoved in his pockets. I let my hand fall to my side and shrugged. "It's just making me...uncomfortable? That's not the right feeling. I don't know what it is exactly, but I don't need anything. I promise. I'm so happy, and the only thing upsetting me right now is you being upset."

Lorne started walking and it took me a few steps to catch up. I felt like the worst kind of jerk. Why couldn't I just take the damned earrings? Why couldn't I just say *sure, Lorne? Those are pretty. Buy them.*

But that felt like lying and I couldn't lie to him. Sure, I could keep things from him, especially things that might hurt him somehow. But I couldn't outright lie.

"I'm sorry. I really did have fun eating with you and trying all those things."

He stopped then and looked down at me. There was too much swimming in his eyes that I needed to process. Love. Sorrow. Guilt. More love.

"You don't need to apologize to me, Amihanna. I love you." He pressed a fist to his heart. "I love you." He let out a breath. "It hurts me to know how hard your life has been, and I know you don't want to talk about it. I *feel* that from you. I know it's not because you don't want me to know, but because it's hard to talk about." He pulled his hands from his pockets and reached a hand to my face. He skimmed a finger down my cheek. "But one day, we will talk about it. Somewhere more private. I want to know *everything*, not just bits and pieces. I think not knowing is making me a little crazy. I want to fix what happened, but I can't. It's too late. So, I want to make up for it."

"You have nothing to make up for." When he tried to talk again, I shook my head. "And knowing everything will make you so, so angry. There's very little good that happened to me the last thirteen years. It's… it's like how you didn't want to tell me what that asshole said in the High Council meeting. It's like that. Knowing the details would only break your heart. Don't you think we've both had enough of that?" I sure thought so. "I want to finish having a nice, lovely time like we did earlier. When we were eating. I want to go back to that. Can we do that?"

Ashino stepped forward and said something softly to Lorne.

Lorne studied Ashino for a second, and then me. And then he said something to Ashino.

That was so annoying. I wasn't going to dig my translator out for that when they knew they were being rude. "What?"

Lorne studied me again. "Ashino wants you to buy something, too, so he was trying to offer some suggestions. He's angry about your past."

"He is?"

"He's been my guard for a long time."

He had? From before Liberation Week? Ashino didn't seem old enough for that. He didn't have any gray in his hair and zero wrinkles. "How long exactly?"

"He remembers you, even if you don't remember him, and he said you always liked to buy things for other people. You used to be a shopper, which is why this is upsetting me so much. This... our trips to markets used to go a lot differently."

"Oh." Should I apologize for another thing that I couldn't remember?

"You bought Ashino something once," he said before I could think of what to say.

I turned to Ashino. He was tall and thicker with muscle than the average Aunare, but that didn't mean much. All the royal guards were built bigger. His eyes were a bright blue, his skin a little darker than mine, and his hair was jet black and long, down-his-back long. It had a few braids at the temples and then tied back in one long tail. I studied his face for a moment. The square jaw. The long nose. The thick black eyebrows that seemed to make his blue eyes brighter.

But no matter how long I stared, I didn't remember him. At all. Not even a glimmer of a memory. "I knew you?"

He nodded. "You bought me this when you were little." He pulled out a little knife and flicked it. The blade opened and was glowing. "I'd just joined Lorne's guard when... but you gave me this before. You said it was for good luck." He tucked the blade away and slid it back into his pocket. "You were always buying things when you were little. Rarely for yourself. But you liked buying gifts."

It was a little unsettling when I realized someone knew me from before. I didn't have memories of back then, but they did. It was like they held this secret bit of me that I couldn't access, and I wasn't sure how to feel about it.

"I have an idea." Lorne's voice pulled me out of my own thoughts. "Come on. This way."

He wove through the stalls, quicker now than we'd moved before.

"Where are we going?"

"You'll see." He kept moving—barely pausing when people bowed or called his name—until we reached a massive stall. It was so big that "stall" was too small of a word. Whoever owned it had actually taken four stalls at the end of an aisle and made a square. Each table had display cases and jars, all filled with brightly colored things of all shapes and sizes. I was sure it was some kind of food because I saw the person before us eating something from it, but I didn't know what kind of food.

"What is it?"

"Candy."

Holy shit. That was a mountain of sugar. "What's that?" I pointed to a jar filled with little balls of every color I could think of, sometimes swirled together, sometimes solidly one color, some of them even glittered. Could you eat glitter?

"Guess we'll have to buy them and see." Lorne grinned like he'd won.

I wanted to argue that we had plenty of food and treats at the estate, but I was curious.

"Don't worry about the money. I promise you have plenty. They can arrange payment through Roan, and if you don't feel comfortable with Roan accessing your accounts, you can hire someone to handle just that bit for you. And even if you didn't have a fortune in your accounts, I do."

"I know. I know. It's just—"

"Hard to part with it when you're used to just surviving."

"No. It's not even that. I'm not hoarding it for when shit goes bad. That's not it."

"Then what is it?"

"It's like I forget it's even there. I haven't earned it, so it doesn't feel real to me. I'm okay with the stuff at the estate. It kind of just shows up so I don't have to think about cost all the time. But I don't feel like I can afford the treats when I know there's a stocked pantry at home."

Lorne's eyes closed for a second. I knew I'd hurt him. I was trying to explain, but I kept making things worse.

When he opened his eyes again, he seemed a little sad. "The money is there and it's yours, but I'm trying to put myself in your spot and understand better. It's difficult for me, but I'm trying. But just like with the food, anything we spend at the market is actually a help to the owner. Not just for the money, but for the attention it'll bring to their stall."

Oh shit. All the air went out of my lungs as the weight of what I'd unknowingly done hit me. "So, I was actually insulting and hurting every other stall we passed."

"No. I gave an excuse at every stall, and I did actually buy you a pair of earrings."

I shoved him softly. "My ears aren't even pierced."

"We could fix that if you want or they can go in the safe or you can give them to your mother. I don't care. But I was done with waiting for you to pick something out." He gave me a sheepish grin. "I couldn't help it."

I rolled my eyes and turned back to the candy. Lorne came to stand next to me, so close that our arms touched.

I leaned into him. "You know, if we got a bunch of things, I could give everything to Roan. And then he could tell me which ones were actually good."

"I could tell you which ones you'd like."

I nudged him. "Yeah, but that's not as much fun as making Roan eat nasty stuff."

Lorne laughed. "All right. So, we'll get a selection?"

"Yeah. For Roan."

"Of course. For Roan." Lorne leaned down, brushing a kiss on top of my head. "But I'll have him put a few for us in a separate bag."

I nodded. "Okay."

But once the guy started ringing up the bags of candy, I started to panic a little. "It's too much," I said to Lorne.

He gripped me by the shoulders and bent forward so that we were eye to eye. "No. It's really not. I haven't gotten to spoil you for thirteen years, and I have a lot to make up for. So, please. Help me out a little. Let me buy you some things today. Or buy things for your friends. Or anyone you feel might need something. Just let me do this. Please."

There was something about his tone—a desperation that made my heart ache with his pain.

And so I swallowed down the anxiety of spending money.

He was the High King. This was good for the man selling him the candy. It was okay to buy something.

"Okay."

Lorne stared at me for a second, and then he stood upright and spoke to the man running the stall.

The candy man quickly turned, bagged something separate, and handed it over.

Lorne took it and turned back to me. "This used to be your favorite."

I opened the bag. Inside was a single little bright yellowish-orange cube that was soft and a little sticky. I took a bite and then grinned. "Melon! It's melon flavored."

Lorne grinned. "It is. Yes." All the sad in his eyes was instantly gone, and now I felt like I'd won.

I handed him back the bag. "More, please."

I thought Lorne would just take the bag, but instead he wrapped his arms around me, and pulled me in for a long kiss.

If I'd been able to think about anyone else, I would've been embarrassed by kissing him like this in public, but I couldn't.

I couldn't think.

I wrapped my hands around his neck, lost myself in the feel of his lips against mine, his tongue against mine, his hands in my hair.

I was breathless when he pulled away just enough to rest his brow on my forehead.

"Thank you," he said.

"For what? The kiss?" I licked my lips. "No problem, but you started it."

He closed his eyes and huffed a soft laugh. "No. That, too. But I meant for asking for more candy."

I placed my hand on his cheek and his eyes opened. All I could see was love and happiness and safety—always safety—in his aquamarine gaze. "I'm sorry. I feel like I keep hurting you, but I honestly don't mean to."

"I know you don't, and none of it's your fault. I just happen to truly love you, and when I know the extent of your hardship… it's not an easy thing for me to let go of." He stepped back, handed the bag back to the candy guy who was smiling at us as if we'd just made his year. People were starting to gather around his stall, waiting for us to finish so that they could buy whatever we were buying. A few were taking pictures, but I tried to ignore them.

Lorne said something in Aunare, and the man hurried to fill a much larger bag. It was clear and as big as my head, and part of me wanted to say no. That was more sweets than I'd ever had in my entire life, but the part of me that wanted the candy won.

I held my hands out for it, but Lorne lifted it just out of reach. "You'll make yourself sick on these, so only a few."

I gave him my best pout.

"Okay, more than a few, but seriously, Amihanna. Not too many."

I gave him a salute. "Sure thing." I held out my hand, wiggling my fingers. "Mine, please."

Lorne handed it over, and I quickly opened the bag. As I popped another melon candy into my mouth, I looked around the market.

Okay, Lorne was hurting because he wanted to buy things for me, and I kept refusing. But maybe shopping wasn't so bad. Relationships were about compromise, and so tonight I would compromise. I'd try doing this his way, and it was a bonus that anything I bought would benefit the owners in multiple ways. Which was a good thing. A very good thing.

I just had to let go of my past and enjoy the moment.

I could do that.

I popped another candy.

Where did I want to go next?

I scanned the market and popped two more into my mouth.

There was a candle stand not far off. Audrey once said she liked candles. I'd met Audrey on Abaddon. She'd been my medic there, and now she was one of my closest friends. She always moaned about how I would've felt better with the nanos if she was burning a soothing candle. That was complete crap because nothing—*nothing*—would've made those tiny bots running through my veins, ripping me apart from the inside to repair the damage to my body feel even remotely better. But clearly she thought so.

Maybe I could get her something from there for when she got back from her trip.

I popped two more candies in my mouth, and then the bag was yanked from my hands.

I glanced up to see Lorne shaking his head at me. "Like a child with this candy still? Even after all these years *and* my warning?"

Ashino was the first to laugh, and then the candy man

laughed. And then the people now lining up around the stall to buy candy started laughing, and from there it spread to everyone in the market.

Oh man. This was embarrassing. "I didn't have that many."

"In the last thirty seconds, you downed six." Lorne bent down and brushed a kiss against my lips. "You're not to be trusted with these," he said as he stood.

I tried to reach around to sneak them from his grip, but he tossed them to Ashino.

"Come on, Ashino." I gave him a wide-eyed look that I thought might soften him up. "Just a few more." Those candies were addictive. The perfect soft but chewy and sweet but with a tang. I could've eaten that whole bag.

Ashino gave me a look like he wanted to give it back. He sighed and reached into the bag, but Eshrin ripped it from his hands.

"These really will make you sick. It's too much concentrated melon with too much sugar." Eshrin glanced at the bag. "His majesty went overboard. This is enough to last you at least a turn around the suns."

Ashino threw me a couple candies, and I laughed. "I knew I liked you."

Lorne shook his head at me but he was smiling like the happiest idiot on Sel'Ani.

I shoved the candies into my mouth before he could think about taking them from me. "That's it," I said around a full, candy-stuffed mouth. "That's all." I started to move through the market, but Lorne picked me up and threw me over a shoulder.

I swallowed the candy, and then hit his back. "Put me down."

"I saw something you might like over here. I'll put you down when we're far away from the candy."

I relaxed into his hold. Giggles followed us as we walked, but I didn't mind. I was having too much fun.

I'd had so many hard nights. So many scary nights when I wasn't sure I'd live to see morning, but tonight was a good one.

Tonight was a really good one.

So, I was going to let Lorne push me out of my comfort zone and buy some things. Because surviving meant living, and damn it, I'd worked hard to get to this point.

To be here, safe, with the man I loved, who loved me.

This was life, and I was going to enjoy it.

I'd earned it.

CHAPTER TWELVE

AMIHANNA

BY THE TIME we decided to head home, I'd become quite the shopper.

I'd gotten a few candles for Audrey. She was due back in two days with Tyler—who had been a prisoner with us on Abaddon, but was now her boyfriend—and I couldn't wait to see her. It felt like too much had happened while she was away, but I was glad she'd taken time to see her extended family. I wanted to have something for her when she got back, and now I did.

And once I found stuff for other people, I started to find a few things for myself—some pocket weapons, a cool ring that was shaped like a firedrake. For some stupid reason, I thought the firedrake had Lorne's smile but no one else saw it. Ashino pretended to, but he was just being nice.

My favorite purchase was a backpack loaded with hidden pockets and zippers and yet feather light. I already had enough go-bags stuck everywhere, but this backpack was next level and I couldn't leave without it.

And the bracelets. That was another favorite. They were those Lorne had been telling me about that could store power. They were one inch wide and made of some kind of flexible metal. They wrapped around my wrist, hugging it like a second skin. They'd been silvery at first, but by the time the ship landed at the estate, they were glowing with a warm white light. Only a tiny bit of silver was left around the edges.

I held them out for Lorne to see. "Look. They're working."

"*Hmm.*" He tapped the one on my right wrist, and it blinked fast five times. "Good. They're fully charged."

I dropped my hands to my sides. "You don't think it's cheating?"

He gave a nod to some of the security as we entered the estate. "No, it's not cheating. Not unless you use them all the time."

I stared down at them as we walked through the halls, winding our way to our suite. "So, should I take them off?"

"You can now that they're fully charged. These you should store for later, but you can put on the other pair we bought when you're doing something that might cause you to lose control. For most people, the bracelets would syphon off enough power to make sure they're not dangerous, but honestly, you have so much inside you that if you really lost control, they wouldn't help that much."

"Oh." That was disappointing. "Then, what's the point?"

We passed one of the kitchen maids—I couldn't remember her name, but I was pretty sure it started with a D. Or maybe it was a B? *Shit.* I needed to get better about remembering the names of the staff.

I raised my hand to give her a quick wave, which made her stumble for a step.

Whoops. Maybe I should've nodded like Lorne, but that felt weird.

Lorne raised a brow, which told me he'd noticed the exchange and he was laughing on the inside.

"Shut up," I whispered to him.

His aquamarine eyes were glittering with laughter, and I poked his side. "Back to the bracelets."

"Whatever you want." He took the next right, and I recognized the hallway. Almost to our suite.

"The bracelets are really for anyone who is weak in power."

"Which I am not." So what was the deal? "I'm confused. I thought they'd save my power so that I could use it later, but also keep me from blowing everyone up."

"Yes. Exactly."

"But... that's not a weak power kind of thing." I was so confused.

"They're not just for someone with fighting abilities. They're not a weapon. They were designed to help any Aunare get a little power boost." He paused for a second to nod to someone who bowed to us.

Was I supposed to nod, too?

No. That was totally for him. I didn't need to.

Did I?

Shit. I was going to have to ask Lorne about that later.

"For instance," he started again, as if the whole bow-nod thing and my awkwardness to acknowledge it never happened, "say you're a cook who's not as good as Nori, but wants to be better. They might activate their *fao'ana* when they're just sitting around wearing those." He tapped the one inch piece of flexible metal wrapped around my wrist. "That power will get stored in the bracelet, and when it's maxed out, the bracelet will start to glow. Like yours are now. Then, they take them off. When they're cooking and need that extra bit to push them from good to great, they put them on. Suddenly they have that little extra to make them great. It's temporary, but it's a way people of lesser power can have a bit more."

"But I have a lot of power."

"Yes. So for you, we want you to have them empty when you're about to lose control. It'll take away some of the power, but if you truly lose it, you could fill up twenty bracelets and not make a dent."

"So, they're useless?" Because I wasn't about to put on twenty sets of these bracelets. That wasn't practical at all.

"No." He gave my shoulder a reassuring squeeze. "Not at all. I wouldn't have bought them for you if I thought they were useless. I think they'll give you a little extra time to gain your balance whenever you're out of control. Think of them as a warning. If they suddenly go from dull to glowing in one instant, it's probably time to take a walk. It's also a good idea to keep a few stored with your power. Because if you're in a fight and start to strobe, then the bracelets could save your life."

"But I shouldn't wear them when I train with you or my guards?"

"No. Because when you're there, you're safe. And you need to learn how to regulate your power without the bracelets. In that way, they could become a crutch."

Okay. That makes sense. "Got it."

"Since these are charged, we'll save these for a fight. The other ones we bought, you can either carry them with you or give them to Eshrin, and put them on when you're about to lose it. Either way, when it's time for the next High Council meeting, having them handy might not be a bad idea."

"Right." The next High Council meeting. That killed my mood instantly.

I didn't like thinking about going to another one, let alone remembering that it might be a daily event.

There were definitely some things that I liked about having this job. The biggest one was getting to marry Lorne. I wasn't sure what the rest were exactly, but I knew something would show up and make ruling worth it.

Maybe.

Ashino stopped us before we entered the suite.

"Yes?" Lorne asked.

"You have company. I was alerted when we arrived."

Company? I looked at my wrist unit. I had to be up early if I was going to get in a decent workout before all the meetings Roan had on my schedule. "Who?" I asked.

"Your father."

I glanced at Lorne. "This is probably going to be bad news. Right?"

Lorne shrugged. "Maybe not, but it doesn't seem good." He pressed his hand to the security panel, and the door to the suite whooshed open.

I didn't know my father well enough to be able to read his moods, but he was sitting on the couch watching the vid screen. I glanced over at it and saw nine different stations playing, which was how Lorne and I usually watched it. Only one station had sound, but it was Aunare and I didn't understand anything other than their tone. A picture of me was next to Captain ni Eneko's on some of the stations, and I was suddenly confused.

Were they trying to say that I'd had a romantic relationship with him? That was absurd, but I wouldn't put it past them to spread a lie like that.

I glanced at Lorne, but his expression was suddenly blank. His king mask was firmly in place.

Okay. That wasn't great. "What's happened now?"

"The press has somehow found out that you'll be training a team with Captain ni Eneko to take down SpaceTech spies, and they're mad," Lorne said.

What? "How could they be mad about me protecting them? That's insane. Isn't that my job?"

"Yes," Lorne said.

My father shot him a look. "No."

I wanted to laugh or scream or something, but none of that would help. Instead, I placed my hands on my hips and waited for more of an explanation.

When nothing came after a minute, I stood in front of the screen. "Well? Who's right?"

"We both are." My father paused all the channels with one Aunare command. "They're saying that it's not the job of the

High Queen, but that's not exactly right. For the last three generations, the High Queen has been a consort to the High King. So, queen in name only. He rules. They've been a figurehead. The Aunare are unhappy with the queen taking risks with her life, but that's not you or what your queenship will look like. You and Lorne are like the kings and queens of old—sharing every responsibility because, unlike the last three High Queens, that's what you're *fao'ana* show. It seems as if they've forgotten our past, our history, and how much it benefits them to have a true High Queen. "

Oh, that was truly insane. "So, I'm not fit to rule. Not fit to marry him. But they don't want me fighting. And all of this before I've even done anything with Captain ni Eneko." Something was seriously off with that reasoning. "No. This is bull. Someone is scared. They don't want to be found."

My father nodded. "Yes. That's exactly right, but it almost doesn't matter because now everyone is in agreement about you becoming High Queen as a consort only. The talk of you is consuming the news and—"

"And it's a good thing that none of this matters," Lorne moved across the room to sit on the couch. He plopped his feet on the ottoman, relaxed back, and it would've seemed like he didn't care, except his skin was suddenly glowing bright.

Damn it.

A big part of me didn't care what any of the reporters were saying, but there was this other side that worried.

I wasn't sure what kind of ruler I wanted to be or how I would contribute—other than by fighting—but if they didn't even want that, if they didn't want me working with Captain ni Eneko to help protect them, then what was left?

I wasn't sure I wanted the job where I just sat next to Lorne and went along with whatever he said. That wasn't me. I couldn't do that.

"The High Council is calling a meeting with you—without Amihanna there—to discuss what she can and cannot do."

For a moment, it was like all the air in the room was sucked into deep space. I couldn't breathe. There was nothing to breathe because if they did that, then I'd have no freedom. No freedom to fight, to protect, to rule. No freedom to be me.

No. This couldn't happen.

I forced myself to find some air. It wasn't done yet. I could still stop this from happening, and maybe it wasn't even something to worry about.

But the way Lorne's skin brightened a little more told me either it was true or else it really pissed him off.

I tapped Lorne's feet, and he moved them from the ottoman so that I could sit on it across from him. "They can't tell me what to do. Can they?" I stared into Lorne's eyes, hoping for something from him that would make this okay, but I didn't see anything good. "I'm not great at following rules. Especially ones I don't believe in."

"I'll fix this," Lorne said.

I wanted to ask how, but something about Lorne's tone worried me. I wasn't sure what he was going to do, and I wasn't sure I wanted to know. Otherwise, I might try to stop him, and that probably wouldn't help me.

I should let him fix it, and yet, that wasn't how I wanted us to work. Judging from the cold look he was giving the vid screen, I was pretty sure that waiting a few minutes to bring that up would be best.

From the way my father moved in slow, deliberate steps to block the screen, I knew I was right to wait.

"Lorne." My father's tone held a soft warning. "It would be best for everyone if you—"

"I appreciate your concern, Rysden, but I'm not worried." Lorne's gaze slid from the vid screens to my father to me, where they lingered. "They'll learn who she is with time, and with time they will accept her. They will know what we see in her and why she will rule."

I looked at my father, but his face was blank. He was too

good at that for me to even attempt to read him. It was almost as if my father had two sides. The one who laughed at the dinner table while I was eating worms, and this other man. This cold man who seemed incapable of emotions.

But I knew that was wrong. If he was this stony, then that had to mean he was truly angry and didn't want to show it.

At least I hoped that was right. I wasn't sure I wanted to be related to someone who could flick off all emotions with a switch.

Lorne turned off the vid screens with one quick command, and I wished it was so easy to turn off all the questions I had in my mind.

"How are we going to turn this around?" I asked.

My father's gaze darted to me and his eyes widened just a little, as if to warn me away from saying anything more.

But I wasn't so good at listening to warnings. Not when I needed to say something. "You guys seem to be upset about the news and the High Council calling a meeting, but I'm not as worried about that. Not when I have to wonder who told the press about the meeting with Captain ni Eneko and the fact that I'm now being used as a distraction. If I'm too busy in High Council meetings, then I won't be looking for whoever is afraid of being found. I can't let that happen."

Lorne was quiet for a long moment and then his skin started to dim. "You're right. I get angry, and I... but you're right." Lorne rose from his spot on the couch.

"This is a distraction we don't need." I kept my calm, in command, even though it felt like everyone and everything was against us. "So, we'll hunt down the spies. We will find who is leaking information to the media and twisting it against us, and we will get rid of them."

"We will, and I think when we do, the people will see what I see." He stepped closer to me. "I want you to have time to learn how to be a leader, and I'm going to give you as much time as possible. But you're right. This—" he waved a hand at the vid screens, "—is a distraction. Not just for the Aunare, but for us. So, you have to shut out all that and do your job."

"And what is my job exactly?"

"To lead. To fight. To command our people. We will do it together." Lorne turned to my father. "It's late. We'll meet in the morning, but for now, let's call it a night."

My father pressed his fist to his heart. "Goodnight, your majesty." Then he turned to me. "I am proud of you. No matter what anyone else says. I hope you know that."

My father gave me a compliment?

I was pretty sure that's what he'd done, and it was nice. It wasn't like he was always critical of me or really said much about what I did or didn't do, but over the last couple of days, he'd started to slip in compliments here and there.

I didn't need his approval, but having it meant a lot. It was more than I could wrap my head around, especially right then.

I knew I wanted to say something, but before I could think of anything, he was gone.

Lorne put his arm around me, leading me through the suite to our rooms. "Are you okay?"

"I think so." I tried to take a quick inventory, but so much had happened today. From the failure of the High Council meeting, to training—complete with mini-meltdown over Eshrin's offhand comment, to meeting with Captain ni Eneko, to our date, and now this... I wasn't even sure what I felt.

There was something I was missing—something bothering me—but I couldn't find the words.

I kept trying to figure it out while I changed into a pair of shorts and loose tank made from the same silky material and got ready for bed, but it was like there were too many thoughts bouncing around in my head. I couldn't catch any of them. It left my head feeling fuzzy and gave me a faint buzzing in my ears.

At my bathroom counter, I finished brushing the fancy braids out my hair that Almya had put in, but I still couldn't grasp any one thought. "Something's wrong. I can't seem to process every-thing that happened today. I think I'm—"

Lorne cut me off by hugging me tight, resting his chin on top of my head. "You're exhausted. You have to be because I know I am." He pulled away, and I looked into his eyes, searching for answers.

And I didn't find them.

But I did find love.

He pressed his lips to mine, and the worry and the fears and that feeling of I-don't-know-what faded away, and all that was left was him.

His hands reached under my tank, and I raised my arms, letting him pull it off me.

He tugged it slowly, slowly up, up, up and over my head, and then from one second to the next, we were both undressed, on the bed, my skin tingling everywhere we touched. Glowing so bright that it hurt my eyes.

I ran my hands down his stomach and wondered how this was possible. How I'd found this kind of happiness.

He gripped my hips and his thumb caressed my tattoo. The one of his firedrake. "I love that you have this."

I laughed. "I'm not obsessed with you." He thought the fact that I'd branded his emblem on my skin meant that I was a big fan, but that wasn't why.

I actually had no idea why, except that maybe a small, hidden part of me remembered him.

He grinned. "Yes, you are completely obsessed with me. Admit it" He moved to hover over me, and I felt him against me and I wanted more. I wrapped my legs around his hips and I felt him press against me, and then away. There and gone.

"Stop it."

"Admit it."

He was teasing me and I couldn't help but love every bit of him. "Okay. I'm obsessed with—"

He kissed me and as he slipped into me I gasped.

It was too much. This feeling of love and contentment grew until it nearly consumed me, and I knew that no matter what we faced tomorrow and the next day and ten years from now, it would be okay.

Because we were together. And when we were together, it was like my soul was whole again.

I never realized how broken I was until I'd found him, but I was okay.

I was better than okay.

His fingertips slipped up my ribcage, spreading warmth through my body, and I gasped. "You still with me?" he asked.

All I could see were his aquamarine eyes as they stared down at me, and I knew whatever happened, everything was going to be all right.

I reached up, pulling him down closer to me so that I could kiss him. "Your eyes are still my favorite color. That's how obsessed I am."

His already bright skin brightened a little more as he pulled away, searching my face. "They are?"

"Yeah. I don't think that's ever going to change." I was with him. I was with him for whatever came next.

And I would find a way through whatever came at us.

He cupped my face in his hand. His thumb brushed back and forth against my cheek.

I leaned into the warmth of his hand but didn't look away from his eyes. I gave him a small nod because I wouldn't lie. Especially about that. Especially not right now, when we were together and so close it felt like we were inside the same skin.

"I love you," I said because I had to. The feelings I had for him were building up to be too much for me to hold inside, and I didn't want to hold them.

His skin lit bright. Like a beacon of his love for me had lit him from within.

He didn't need to say the words—I could see them in his eyes —but he said them anyway. "I love you." He muttered something in Aunare, and I wasn't sure what it meant, but I knew it was good.

He began to move again, and I wanted to ask him what he'd said, but everything disappeared except me and him and us and wave after wave of feeling until I couldn't do anything but surrender to him.

And he was good.

He was better than good.

He was amazing.

CHAPTER THIRTEEN

AMIHANNA

I WAS LYING in bed hours later, drifting somewhere between awake and asleep, listening to Lorne sleep peacefully beside me, and trying to ignore that feeling creeping back into my mind.

Something was wrong. Something about what was happening right now was wrong, and yet there was so much happening that I couldn't figure out what was bothering me specifically or how to fix it.

If I didn't know what it was, how could I fix it?

I wasn't going to be able to sleep until whatever was brewing in my subconscious bubbled to the surface.

My mind drifted through everything that had happened during the day—watching the people watch me at the market, the news reports, and going over the meeting with the High Council. I wasn't sure what made it click, but finally, after way too long lying there, a realization hit me. I knew why I was so upset.

I hadn't had a second alone to think about how to get the Aunare to approve of my rule—and this war—but the more I lay there and tried to think of a solution, the more complex the problem became.

I'd promised Lorne I would fix this, but I was starting to think that it wasn't fixable.

But I wouldn't give up. I would find a way.

There had to be a way. Earlier—for a fraction of a second at the market—I had an idea, only I couldn't remember it now.

I glanced at Lorne. His face was relaxed and at peace. His dark hair spread across the pillow, and his arm was reaching out toward me, as if even in his sleep he was drawn to me.

I shifted a little farther away from him, not because I wanted to, but because if I didn't, I would never get out of this bed. And I had to. I would. I just needed a few seconds to get my body to move.

I had to fix this, and not just because I'd promised Lorne I would. There were so many reasons why I needed the Aunare to not just accept me, but to rally for what was going to come next. I couldn't keep being afraid of assassination attempts from the Aunare, even if that fear of attack was pretty familiar. I knew I couldn't make the Aunare like me, but I needed them to accept me as a ruler because war was coming. Whether they wanted to ignore it or pretend it was my fault or whatever. They needed to *see*.

That seemed insane because I didn't even know what I was supposed to be doing, but somehow, I had to make them believe I was not just up to the job, but I was going to be the frostiest High Queen they'd ever seen.

I wanted to wake up Lorne and ask for help, but he couldn't. Not even a little bit. Not with this.

I let out a harsh breath as I studied his profile. This man loved me so much that he might actually be making it worse. He didn't understand why the Aunare didn't like me, and worse— he was intolerant of anyone speaking against me. Which I understood to some extent. If someone was talking about him the way they were about me, I probably wouldn't even be able to think coherently. I'd just want to ice them all. That had to be why he was on this *you have no choice, I will force you to love her or else* kick.

It wasn't helping. He wasn't helping. But I knew someone who might.

I slid out of bed and froze, watching Lorne while I held my breath. When he didn't wake up after a minute, I knew he probably wouldn't. But I still had to be careful.

I tiptoed to our bathroom, and then through to the closet. I grabbed a pair of leggings and one of Lorne's supersoft sweaters and tugged them on, then kept moving.

Deep in the back of the closet, behind a row of clothes, was a door. The door led into another room. My old room. The one I had when I was a child.

I pushed the clothes aside and pushed down the little door. It was for little-me so I ended up crawling through it.

I slipped out of the adjoining closet, into the empty suite, then out of the suite and into the hall. The lights were dim and, since the estate had been shut for the night, the estate's security team was on duty while my guards slept. I knew some of Lorne's were in the security room watching the cameras, but they wouldn't wake him for this. Eshrin would probably get an alert that I was up and moving, but hopefully he'd just keep an eye on where I went and go back to sleep.

Because I wasn't going far.

I moved quickly through the family wing to Roan's room and pressed my hand on the panel. There was a faint click and then the door *whooshed* open.

I waited one step inside the door for my eyes to adjust to the dark again. It took a second, but then I could make out his small room—the tiny kitchenette off to the side next to the window, the large bed with two side tables, and then the sitting area with two chairs and a small table.

I couldn't make out any odd lumps on the floor, which was surprising. I waited another second just in case my eyes hadn't adjusted enough, but no, his floor was clear. On Earth, Roan was usually a fraction of a degree tidier than I was, but that wasn't saying much.

I took one last look around, and then realized I was an idiot. The house staff must've cleaned recently, which meant no hazard of tripping over anything. Lorne would be so annoyed at me if I busted an ankle sneaking into Roan's room.

I crossed quickly to the bed and sat next to him. "Roan," I whispered.

He didn't move or make a sound.

I tapped his shoulder. "Roan," I said a little louder.

He wrapped his arm around my waist and tugged me on top of him. "What's up, baby?" His words were slurred with sleep.

I froze in horror, splayed across him, before I shoved him.

He responded by wrapping a leg around my hips.

"Gross." I shoved until I was free of him, then perched on the edge of the bed again.

Roan reached for me again, and I punched his shoulder—not hard, but with enough force to wake him up. "*Roan.*"

"What?" He sat up, blinking his eyes, searching the room blindly. "What's happening?"

I stood and ordered the lights on dim. "Roan, I need you to wake up."

"Am?" He rubbed a hand down his face. "What the hell time is it?"

"Just after four in the morning."

"Was there an attack?" He sat up straighter and threw the covers off himself.

I had a second to cringe before I realized he was wearing pants. I never knew what I was going to get when it came to Roan. More than once I'd seen too much and it was awful. I mean—I was pretty sure other girls would disagree, but I didn't need to see it.

"Is everyone okay? Were there any—"

"No attack. Sorry." I held out a hand to stop him getting up.

"I was about to freak out if you were naked under those covers, but—"

"You wish I was naked." He ran a hand down his bare chest.

I gagged, dramatically. "Been there and gross. Just yuck."

"Admit it. I'm just more than you could handle."

I couldn't help it. I had to laugh at his stupid smile.

"And hey, getting tangled up in bed with me when you wake me up is so much better than your reaction. I mean, if I reacted like you, I could've killed you."

Now that made me really laugh. "Sure you could've."

"Shut up." His grin faded, and he studied me for a second. "Seriously, Am. What the fuck is going on? Why are you in my room this early?"

I blew out a breath. "I need your help. I'll get the *wyso*." I knew he had some chilled in his small kitchenette. "But you have to wake up."

He groaned. "I'd been having a really good sex dream..." He grabbed his tablet from his bedside table, and then leaned back against his pillows.

Good. He was awake enough that I could leave him for a second and not awake enough to finished telling me all about his dream. I moved across the room to the kitchenette and grabbed down two glasses.

"I don't have any alerts. Nothing's going on. Did you have a nightmare?"

"No. Nightmare would require sleep, and I haven't had any."

"Oh shit."

I spun to look at him. "What?"

"Did you and Lorne have a fight? You guys can't fight. It'd be like—"

"Roan. Calm down." I rolled my eyes at him. "I just need your help with something. Let me get the caffeine going so we can talk like normal people."

"You did not wake me up for some shenanigans. We don't have time in your schedule for—"

I gave up trying to respond to him because the man wasn't listening. Instead, I poured two glasses and walked over to him, handing him one. When he finally stopped rambling to take a sip, I started over. "There's something I need to talk through with my best friend, and I don't have time with you anymore— or not enough time. So, can you just be my best friend right now?"

"Okay." He took another sip. "Best friend mode activated. What's on your mind at this ungodly hour of the morning?"

I moved to his little sitting area and curled up in one of the chairs. "They hate me."

Roan followed me and sat in the opposite chair. He set his glass down with a *thunk*. "Who gives a shit what they think?" He didn't need an explanation. He just knew.

"I do." I needed him to understand. He was my best friend. By best friend law, he had to understand. "I have to rule these people, and I can't do that if they hate me and question everything I do. It won't end well. When people don't believe or trust their leaders… it'll be just like SpaceTech to the Earthers. I can't do that. I can't be that. And eventually, they'll revolt. They'll have to."

"They might not revolt." Roan leaned back in his chair. "This isn't like Earth and you're not a fucking Murtagh, Am. You're new to them, and they might—"

Ice it all. He was just as bad as Lorne. I knew exactly where that sentence was going. "Okay. Fine. They might eventually change their mind, but that's not a given. And I can't ask the Aunare to risk their lives in this war if they don't even believe I should rule." I set down my untouched glass of *wyso*. I was too worked up to add any caffeine that might amp it, especially on no sleep.

I had to move if I was going to think this through. I started pacing. "I don't know what I can do to make them see that I'm up for this job. I passed their stupid test. I defended their city. I told them some of my secrets and why I'm angry at them, and maybe that's the problem. But I already said the words. I can't unsay them." I sat on his bed again. "What do I do?"

Roan nodded. "You need an Aunare perspective on this. Why didn't you ask Lorne?"

I made a face at him.

"Right. You already did, but because he loves you, he thinks everyone else should. And if they don't, then screw 'em." Roan shrugged. "I kind of agree with him." His voice went up at the end, like he expected me to get mad.

Except I wasn't mad. But I was starting to feel defeated.

"Maybe if you didn't watch the news feeds every morning then you wouldn't feel like it mattered."

"But it does matter. We lived on a planet where the general population hated the people that ruled them. It was awful. I don't want that for anyone here. So, what can I do?"

"Give it time."

I snatched his tablet up and used it to turn on his vid screens. Roan's screen was smaller than Lorne's and could only fit half as many channels, but it was early enough for some of the morning feeds from the colonies.

Two of the news stations were talking about how I was a potential spy. Another said I'd tricked Lorne into marriage. Two more were talking about how I was going to destroy the Aunare culture, and that the only answer was to overthrow Lorne.

Overthrow Lorne. Because of me.

No. Not happening. I had to do something. But what?

"Holy shit." Roan drank down more of his *wyso*. "Don't they have something more important to talk about than you?"

"I wish. There's plenty to report on, and yet, they're stuck on me? *Me?*" It was beyond absurd. "But I'm supposed to be the High Queen. So, I get it. Apparently, I'm important."

Roan laughed. "Who'd have thunk it? The scrawny girl from the street was secretly the future High Queen of the Aunare."

"Yeah, I know, right? The absurdity isn't lost on me." I switched them all to mute. "It's insane, but I guess it's true. I need them to approve of me, not just because I want them to like me. I couldn't give a shit. But I need them to follow me into war. I need them not to revolt against Lorne. And I need them to not feel like we did on Earth."

"Okay." Roan set down his empty cup. "You have a point."

"Thank you. So, what do I do? Because I have no ideas and Lorne doesn't even see this as a problem. I was getting an idea of what to do, but now I forgot and I can't—" I stopped talking because it wasn't helping.

"I don't know what we should do, but I see the problem now. I need a second. Let me get dressed and we'll figure it out just like we've figured out everything else."

I nodded. "Okay." I nodded again. "Okay," this time I said it with some relief.

Roan disappeared into the bathroom, and I kept pacing.

Ten minutes later, he came back with damp hair and with his clothes on for the day. Suddenly, I felt underdressed in leggings and Lorne's sweater, but Roan was Roan. I didn't care what I looked like. He'd seen me at my worst, and this wasn't it.

"Any ideas?" I asked, hoping he had something.

"Not really. I don't know. I keep circling back to the whole give-them-time thing. They just need to get to know you and understand that you're not Murtagh. You're not the bad guy. They'll see."

"Maybe." But I needed it to happen faster because we were nearly out of time. War was inevitable, and they needed to be ready.

I needed them to see the truth and understand who I was, and I thought I'd done that. They'd seen me fight for them at Lorne's speech and above their capital city.

I'd taken their test, and while I was there I'd told them—

"Wait." I spun to Roan. "Wait." There it was. The idea. I needed a second.

Roan held up his hands. "Whatever you need. I'm waiting."

I paced for a second longer before I froze.

This was it. This was it.

I turned to Roan. "I have an idea, but…"

He winced, and I knew he knew what I was going to say.

"It could totally backfire, but I mean—can it really get worse than this?" I motioned to the vid screen where information about an uncovered assassination plot was breaking.

"I don't know. I mean, I say no, but we both know that things can always get worse."

Right. That was true. "Okay. Noted."

"But tell me your idea anyway." He sat down again in one of his chairs and motioned me to the other one. "Let's see if there's something there that we can work with."

"Okay." I let out a nervous breath, but I couldn't sit. Instead, I stood next to the chair. "Here's the problem as I see it right now: they don't know me. I ranted a bit—kind of psycho-esque—in the arena, but I didn't give them a chance to really understand. I think there's a disconnect between the truth and what the former High King let them know. And until they really *see* it, they won't get it. Telling them didn't help, and if I put myself in their shoes and someone told me everything I believed was a lie, I might not take their word for it. Especially if that person was a stranger."

"I think I'm getting you." Roan sat back in the chair. "Keep going."

"Lorne was saying something at the market earlier, last night, whatever. That doesn't matter. But he was saying how he was having trouble understanding what it was like for me exactly, and I could see all these questions bubbling inside him. But it wasn't the time or the place to really get into it, but I think it's the same for all of the Aunare. I think they need proof. I think that they need to see what it was like—Liberation Week, all the revolts, the executions. I think I might have to actually *show them* to get them to believe what I'm saying is true."

"Okay. Okay, yeah. I'm with you on that. I can see how that might be true. So, how are you going to show them? Do you want me to arrange a speech or something? Or—"

I sat in the chair, thankful that he was getting on board with my plan. But I should've known he'd agree, not just because he was my best friend, but because he was an outsider like me. "The interview with Himani is coming up in two days. If you could delay it a couple more to give us some time, then I think we could use that. If I came here early in the morning like this, we could pull clips. We'd need to go through all the footage from Liberation Week, from the execution arenas, from that revolt—"

"Oh, babe. There must be so much they don't know. I think I'm so with you on this. They need to see it. There's no way they can watch all of that and not be mad as hell."

A little zing of excitement hit me. "Right? If we showed them —really showed them and explained everything to them about how it all went down—then we can make all of the Aunare *see*."

"Babe. You're thinking too small. We get this streamed to everyone. Across the universe. Everyone can tune in at once and no one will mess with your clips if it's streamed live. It'll hit everyone at once. Even Earthers will see it."

The idea of being live to that many people made me want to throw up, but he was right. "Okay. Yes. Live is probably better. But if we do this right, I think we can use this interview to turn around the Aunare's perception of me, of what happened with SpaceTech, and why every single one of them should want this war. Because right now, there's a good portion of the Aunare who are siding with SpaceTech, and that's so beyond fucked up that a million light years can't span the distance."

Roan huffed. "It really is fucked up, right?"

"For sure." It was evil how SpaceTech had murdered so many Aunare and then corrupted the minds of the rest. "The hardest part is going to be finding the right footage to get them to really understand what happened. There's just so much to go through. Most of the original vids—the non-SpaceTech propaganda ones—are going to be on the off-the-grid sites, but we should use some of their stuff, too. The stuff from the original news reports." Oh my God. This was going to take forever. "I don't know. Maybe this is a bad idea. It feels like an impossible task to go through everything and there's no time—"

"No. This is actually really good, and I can help. It's actually not an impossible task, but it'll take some time. We'll start with what you want to say. Let's get that down." He reached for his tablet and started typing as he talked. "And then we'll search for clips to back it up. I can do that when you're training. Get some stuff pulled for you to look at, and then we'll edit it down to fit exactly what you need. We'll make it flow." He looked up at me. "We will show them who you are, the evil that you—and every Aunare in SpaceTech territory—have endured, and we'll show them the truth. By the end of it, they'll be as ready to go to war as you are."

When he broke it down like that, it sounded easy. I wanted to believe him so bad. I was desperate for hope. "You really think we can do all that?"

"I think *you* can. I don't think it'll be easy, and you'll have to open yourself up more than you ever wanted to, but I think if anyone can do it, it's you." He put down his tablet and looked me in the eyes. "Not messing with you. You can do this." That tone? It was something I couldn't ignore. That tone told me he believed those words with everything he had.

"Okay." I didn't like that I had to do this, but I would. I would say what needed to be said. It was time for them to see who I was, why I was this way, and for them to understand that they should be just as angry.

I would make them hear me.

I would make them see.

And when I was done, I would make them stand and fight.

Because evil had already come for us, and it was way past time for the Aunare to show what they could do to stop it.

It was time.

CHAPTER FOURTEEN

AMIHANNA

IN MY TWENTY years of life, there were days when I thought I'd die and days when I was so tired or in pain or without hope that I wished I would die. But now, whole days went by without me ever thinking about dying at all. I was almost getting used to thinking beyond one day at a time, which was a huge step for me.

Except today. Today was going to be a completely iced monkey shit of a day.

Today was the day that Roan and I had been working toward for four days. We'd gone through footage, and I'd practiced what I'd say. I hoped it was enough. I hoped I'd picked the right things that would get through to the Aunare.

Either way, today, right now, I'd give my interview.

There was so much riding on this, and I almost wished I'd shared what I was going to do with Lorne. But I hadn't.

And now it was too late.

Today, I'd show the Aunare who I was, who I would be, and why I wanted to lead them to war.

I would definitely survive this interview, but I desperately wanted to skip over the next few hours. And thinking that made me feel weighted down in piles of thick, murky guilt. I was going so soft that I was complaining about something that wasn't even remotely dangerous. Nothing today would threaten my life.

What were a few unpleasant hours when they could help me change everything?

And still, I was sitting on a loveseat next to Lorne, staring at the man sitting in the chair across from me as if he were my opponent instead of my interviewer because, today, he was.

Himani might not truly be my enemy, but he was one of the Aunare's most famous reporters. Which meant he was really good at uncovering secrets, and I was all too used to holding every secret I had with a death grip.

A death grip that I was about to loosen by choice and calculation.

It was supposed to be a small interview—just me, Lorne, and Himani—but the room was packed. I hadn't been expecting so many people. No one else seemed surprised, so I guessed I was the clueless one here. Way too many people I didn't know were peppering me with questions that didn't matter—like if I was comfortable—which was no, I wasn't. I was about to go live in front of trillions of people across the known universe. After so many years of trying to avoid cameras and being seen, this was a nightmare—to be stared at by countless people while I was forced to reveal myself—so, no, I wasn't comfortable. Not even a little bit.

They kept asking if the lights were too bright. Yes, they were. But that didn't mean that they would turn them down. Because I'd already asked that, and they said no.

But this was my life now. This was my choice. I'd survived too much to back down now. I had to make my life count. I had to make everything I did matter. Starting with this interview.

This was my first step to become the person I wanted to be.

I gritted my teeth to keep from snapping at one of Himani's many assistants. He was swatting at me with a powder puff again. He grumbled in Aunare and when Lorne snapped sharply at the man, I was sure it was a good thing I didn't understand Aunare.

I glanced at Lorne as the dude with the puff scrambled away. "Thanks."

Lorne—skin glowing so soft his *fao'ana* were only just visible—reached out for my hand, and I took it. We were a team. A united front against our enemy. Only a small coffee table with three glasses of water on top separated us from Himani who was patiently waiting to begin the interview.

Himani was older than my father by at least ten years. His white hair was long and intricately braided in two plaits. He sat relaxed in the chair as if all these people—his crew there to record, not to mention his security, and team of assistants—didn't bother him in the slightest. And that wasn't even taking into account my parents standing off to the side, Roan, Fynea,—and then the team of people—both ours and Himani's—who were there to make sure Lorne and I looked our best. Plus, our guards. So many guards.

Himani raised a brow at me—as if to ask me if I was ready to start.

My heart raced and I gave him a tiny shake of the head. I needed a second before we dove in.

I forced myself to breathe evenly as I took in the room, hoping that looking away from everyone staring would help me calm down. A real fire filled the fireplace beside us, giving off crackles and pops as the wood burned. The armchair Himani was sitting in was made from a metallic material that reflected the flickering firelight. And as I looked around the room, I realized that the placement of every knickknack scattered around the room—some of them Earther, some of them Aunare, and some of them altogether different—tried to give the illusion that this was a normal home, a normal interview, and that we were normal people. It tried and failed, at least to me. This interview was supposed to tell the Aunare people how I might act as their queen, which was so far from normal it wasn't even in the same universe. But I needed it to do so much more.

I couldn't rule a people that didn't believe in me. I wouldn't do that to the Aunare. I needed them to understand. I needed them to know. I needed them to see me as the one they wanted to be in command.

"You're going to do great," Lorne said, and I turned to him again.

The simple ring of gold around Lorne's head glinted in the light, and I couldn't help but think about how handsome, official, *kingly* he seemed right now. He tried to convince me to wear one, too, but I refused. I wasn't their queen. Not yet. And I wasn't going to put one on and have them hate me more.

Not when I needed them to see me as I was.

But if I did my job well today, then maybe they'd accept me as their queen. Some might even be glad that I was going to rule.

He squeezed my hand. "You're going to have to start breathing."

I took in a laughing, gasping breath. "Right."

Air was important, but sometimes it was hard for me to remember that when I looked at him. I got lost. The kind of lost where I felt like I was tumbling and falling and spinning, but somehow, it wasn't terrifying. Because he was here with me, and he made me feel safe anywhere. When I was with him, it was almost as if the last thirteen years hadn't happened.

Almost.

Loving him didn't erase the past, but it made it easier.

"You're going to do great," Lorne said again.

"Right," I said again, but this time, I wasn't sure I believed it.

His faith in me and our destiny together was disarming. It made me feel like I was somehow betraying him when I questioned it, but I couldn't help it. I had so many questions about the past and the future that it was hard to focus on the present.

And yet, here I was. About to make everyone face the past that I'd lived and argue for saving the future.

There was a tension in the room that felt very similar to the feeling I got right before a fight. It was nervousness combined with a touch of anticipation and a stubborn, never-give-up need to win. I gripped that feeling tight. I would need it if I was going to get through this.

Because today, right now, I was going to show the Aunare exactly who I was.

I was about to signal that I was ready for Himani to begin, but Lorne changed that with one word.

"Amihanna." The way he said my name—long and drawn out, with a soft comfort in his tone and an understanding of what I was feeling—made everything inside me shift.

My skin was suddenly bright and my *fao'ana*—the symbols on my arms and back—showed not only who I was and what I was capable of, my past, and my fragile destiny. The frenzied, ready-to-fight feeling slipped through my fingers, and all I was left with was a feeling that I needed to hide.

Damn it. That was exactly what I didn't need.

I was wearing a back-baring halter top with no sleeves because Almya said it would be best, and I'd been too scared about how this was going to go to argue with her. The shirt was gorgeous, but it showed too much skin, especially when I was glowing. Clearly the shirt had been a mistake.

"You had to do that now?" I whispered to Lorne. I knew he still wouldn't really understand why I was annoyed. He wore his *fao'ana* with pride, but it was different for me. I truly hated baring so much of my soul on my skin for everyone to see.

Lorne didn't even look a little bit sorry for it.

"You did that on purpose," I murmured quietly to him, aware that even if the cameras hovering around the room weren't broadcasting yet, they might be recording.

"No, it wasn't on purpose, but I would've if I'd thought of it." He took a breath and relaxed his hold on his power. Instantly his skin glowed even brighter. His *fao'ana* that had been dimly on display earlier were now beacons drawing every eye in the room. All talking quieted as the small crowd in the room took in their King.

"Better?" he asked.

"No." It wasn't better for me, but I knew it was better for the interview that we were both showing our true selves to everyone.

One of the many hovering cameras buzzed toward my face. I wanted to walk out of the room, but my stubbornness—and Lorne's grip on my hand—held me in place.

I had a purpose.

I was in command.

I just needed time to make the interview into what I wanted —what I needed.

"Are you ready?" Himani asked.

I gave him a sassy smile even though I was filled with fear and anxiety. "It's probably too late to change my mind now."

Himani laughed, but Lorne turned to me. "It's never too late. You want them gone, they're gone." His tone was sharp, firm, kingly.

My father cleared his throat, and Lorne spared him one glance that put him in his place before focusing on me again.

"It's never too late," Lorne said again, this time soft and heavy with concern.

Oh man. Guilt rose up inside me, making my stomach ache.

It was too late because I had my own plans for this interview. If I was lucky, I was going to fulfill my promise to him today.

I caught Roan's gaze across the room, and he gave me a nod. He thought I should've told Lorne about my plan for today, but I needed Lorne's reaction to be real. I needed this to work more than I needed Lorne's approval. I needed him to step up as much as I needed the Aunare to finally accept—or reject—me as their queen.

"It's okay," I said, glancing back at Himani and going for a lighthearted tone. I almost laughed at the sound of my father's relieved breath. "Everyone's here and ready. We might as well get it over with."

Himani gave a nod to his assistant and red flashing lights lit on the cameras. There were six in total, surrounding me and Lorne and Himani at various angles.

"We'll be live in a moment."

One of the assistants in the back started counting down in Aunare. I knew those words because my guards used them so much when we were training together.

"*Shehsa.*" Five.

"*Uhona.*" Four.

"*Shana.*" Three.

"*Resh.*" Two.

From a place that felt far away, I could hear Himani giving a brief introduction in Earther English, but everything in my mind was quiet as I braced for the first question.

I could do this. I would do this. I would make them hear me so the Aunare would stop making me out to be the villain while ignoring the true evil that was already destroying them.

I would make them hear me so that maybe—just maybe—I could help the halfers and Earthers and Aunare who were stuck on Earth under the rule of an evil corporation.

If I did this right, I could save so many lives. Enough lives that I shouldn't worry about anything other than getting through to the people watching.

Lorne squeezed my hand hard and I realized I'd missed the whole start of the interview.

Time to focus.

I released his hand and tried to act naturally, whatever the heck that meant.

"...Just before we started the live feed, Amihanna expressed that she wasn't thrilled to be doing this interview. So, that's where we'll begin." Himani's gaze darted from the camera hovering in front of him to me. "I don't love thinking that you don't want to do this interview, Amihanna, but that already gives me so many questions to ask." Himani's clover green eyes seemed to glitter with curiosity. "For someone who has claimed to want to rule, you'd have to know that interviews would be part of your regular routine."

Himani had a job that suited his soul and his *fao'ana*. He lived to ask questions and dive deeper into the inner workings of his subjects. But I didn't want anyone diving deep into my head, especially not in front of such a massive audience.

This was going be tricky. Very, very tricky. "That's not a question, and I don't think I've ever said that I wanted to rule. Have I?" I said it teasingly, but it was a serious answer. I never said this was a job I *wanted*. I'd said that it was a job I'd take—partly out of obligation, partly out of love for Lorne. But it wasn't as if I asked to be queen.

The way Himani's skin glowed with my answer told me I might have given him something surprising. "I guess you haven't said that, at least not now that I'm thinking about it. I believe you spoke about your destiny to rule when you were in the arena and about how you weren't sure if the Aunare were worthy of you, but that's something altogether different. Isn't it?"

"It is." I leaned closer to him. "I thought you had a list. One that a bunch of those people over there haggled about for weeks." I motioned behind him to his assistants, and to Roan and Fynea. "I'm not sure any of these questions you're asking me right now are on your list. Are they?"

He gave me a little sheepish grin that made me laugh. "I'm sure you wouldn't mind if I added a few in. Among friends. And I think we can call each other friends after waiting so long for the interview negotiations to conclude."

That was probably the reason why Himani had the following that he did. He asked the questions people wanted answered, not the ones on some stupid list. "I'm sure I wouldn't know the difference. I pretty much ignored everything about those negotiations."

"Amihanna." This time it was my mother hissing my name.

"It's fine, Mom."

Since Roan was one of the hagglers over the list of questions, I knew nothing would be approved that I wouldn't want to answer. Plus, I was about to play a very public game of bait and switch. As soon as Himani gave me a window, I would take over.

But my mother was still giving me *the eye.* "The interview will be more natural if I haven't prepared for it." It was a lie. I had prepared. Just not how she meant. And as excuses went, that one shouldn't have gotten me very far, but Mom nodded like it made sense.

Lorne was quiet next to me, and I wasn't sure if I was doing a good job or if his silence meant something else. But I didn't dare look at him. "What've you got for me, Himani?"

"Going back to that day in the arena when you unexpectedly took the test to become one of the Aunare's most elite warriors—you didn't seem to be shy about anything when you spoke to me that day. You didn't seem to have anything to hide. In fact, I'd say you had more than enough things to say that we hadn't heard before from anyone." He tilted his head a little. "You know, I spent the days and days of negotiations watching everything I could find about you—that arena interview, your short speech in the hallway here after the attack on your father's estate, and all the footage of you on Abbadon, and a few others that I was able to dig up. It's been fascinating getting to see you in action, but the more I watched the more confused I became. It seemed so out of character for you to talk to me in front of so many people. What made you speak up when you were so used to hiding? Was it my questions or that there were so many people there or something else entirely?"

"Your oversize holographic head was in the way," I said flatly.

Himani laughed like I wanted him to.

It was the truth, though. "You didn't really give me a choice. I had to answer your questions, or you wouldn't move."

Himani huffed. "I'll give you that, but that wasn't the case the whole time. You were pretty free with your words that day after our deal was made."

I'd watched the replay of that day, and the whole thing made me cringe. I couldn't point to one thing and say that was why I spilled my guts because it was more general than that. "I think it was mostly anger that made me answer your questions. I guess I was sick of it. I guess I still am."

I saw Lorne stiffen out of the corner of my eye, but I kept my gaze focused on Himani. I wouldn't get through this if I looked at Lorne now.

"Sick of what exactly?" Himani asked.

"Sick of everything." I almost left it at that, but my mother caught my eye and waved her hand in the air in tight circles as if that would somehow will me to keep talking.

Her annoying little Mom move worked.

Fine. "I was sick of everyone assuming how I felt or what I thought. Sick of everyone blaming me for things that weren't my fault while accepting none of the blame themselves." I saw a segue and took it. "But mostly, I was sick of the inaction of the Aunare people. It hit me that day when I was about to watch someone die in an arena *again* that maybe the Aunare didn't care about others' lives enough to take on any risk themselves. That's been the toughest for me to understand about you."

Bait. This was my bait.

"What do you mean?"

"I mean you—and when I say you, I mean the collective Aunare—didn't do anything when SpaceTech started slaughtering your own people. You did nothing for thirteen years. You've done nothing now. How can you do nothing when others are suffering and dying? And then in the next breath, how can you call *me* names, tell me *I'm* unworthy, and point a finger at me saying this war is somehow *my fault*? Even after I saved

Ta'shena? And this morning I got a report on how many assassination attempts might be tried today, and I thought, what did I do to deserve this?"

Himani's eyes went wide, and I was willing to bet good money that his shock was genuine. "I didn't realize it was that bad."

"It's not been very welcoming here, that's for sure. How could it be when assassins want me dead and your colleagues are shouting to anyone that will listen that I'm to blame for the war?" I didn't give him time to respond. "Back to your question, though." I leaned toward him slightly, hoping to draw him closer to where I wanted, as I kept talking. "I guess I was sitting in the arena box that day and watching everyone else do nothing while Ulshan slid closer to death. He was just a man—an honorable officer of the law—trying to earn a better life. That he would die in the arena trying to pass some stupid test? It just pissed me off. I couldn't watch him die. And for the first time, I thought I should do something even though no one else would. I thought maybe that meant I was more Earther than Aunare and maybe that wasn't such a bad thing. As I jumped down into the arena, I wondered if your media was right, and I should leave. Not because of their bogus reasons about me not being fit for the position or worthy or somehow at fault for the war, but because of the way that you were all going to watch Ulshan die. In that moment, I'd lost complete and utter respect for all of you, and if doing nothing was what the Aunare did best, then I wasn't sure I wanted to be Aunare anymore."

There were all kinds of grumbles from everyone in the room, but I wouldn't sit there and lie. It was a bold thing to say, but I was done being quiet. It was time for me to speak. It was time for them to *listen*.

They had to understand now or they would die.

Not by my hand, but by SpaceTech's.

"You don't still think that do you?" Lorne sounded equally hurt and horrified.

"Think what?" I wanted to reach out to him and soothe the hurt, but I couldn't. I had to focus on maneuvering Himani's questions.

"That you don't want to be here, be Aunare, rule with me?"

There wasn't anything in his tone, but his frequencies shifted enough that I reached for his hand. I couldn't stop myself no matter how many people were watching. "I can't leave you. That's not up in the air anymore." I didn't leave any room for questioning that in my tone, and I hoped that eased his heart.

"But?" he asked. "What about the rest of it?"

This was tricky. Trickier than I thought it would be because I didn't want to hurt Lorne, but I had to be honest. "I just..." I wasn't sure how to say it, and this was too important for me to mess up. I needed a second.

After a moment, I began again. "When your father was ruling, I understood that he was manipulating things. I got that. When you became king, you freed the media, and that's changed some of what I'm seeing reported now. You were right. I do see that on the official polling forty-nine point seven percent want me to stay, to marry you, to be queen, but on one station yesterday, that number was only twenty-eight. Which feels pretty low to me. There's a small percentage that are undecided, but there's also a big portion of the Aunare that are loud and angry and dangerous, and for whatever reason, the media is still fueling that anger. What scares me is that some of them will feel forced to have me as their ruler. They didn't choose me. And while that might be something that's normal for the Aunare, I know what it feels like to hate the person who has control over your life. I won't do that. And I don't want to push the Aunare to war and be blamed for it. It's wrong on so many levels. Which means that I can't afford to stay quiet anymore. Not if I can change their minds today. Because that minority has become a mob, and if they can't wake up, if they can't see the truth through the lies, then this war is already lost."

"How are you planning on changing their minds?" Himani asked.

"My words in the arena weren't enough. Some of them are saying I made everything up, which is insanity. But it's also something that I can fix. I'm going to show your viewers what actually happened thirteen years ago and what has been happening since." But it wasn't just that.

This was the part that might upset Lorne.

"None of the Aunare did anything to help us." I turned to Lorne before he could speak. "I know you wanted to, but you didn't." My father started to speak up, and I caught his gaze and shook my head. "Not until it was almost too late to save me. And I could let that go. I could say that it was in the past and we could move forward from here. But we still haven't acted against SpaceTech, even after everything they've done. We're still here, not doing *anything* after a major attack on your capital city, after they destroyed one of your vacation planets, slaughtered thousands of families. They're still murdering your—*our*—people and no one is doing anything."

I turned to Lorne. "You're arguing with your advisors and our allies all day, but even you're not doing anything. I don't want to come at you like this, but I've tried talking to you—" I looked at my father. "—to all of you, and nothing is changing. I don't understand why. I can't see a future down this path for any of the Aunare, and I don't see any hope for the Earthers, and that's making it harder for me to let go of my anger about the past. I know I need to let it go, but I can't. I *can't*."

I looked at Himani. "The Aunare have more tech, more firepower, more people than the Earthers. We can end this war before it really gets going, but I can't be the only one who wants to fight. I can't—I won't—fight alone anymore."

This was it. I was going to change some minds today. I had to. "I'm hoping by my being here, by *showing you*—not just telling you—about my life and my experiences and what happened to all the Aunare on Earth and its colonies, you'll be ready to take on this war with me instead of blaming me for it."

"No one should blame you for anything." Lorne's voice was cold and quiet, but I could feel the hum of his anger simmering. I hoped it was anger at the war or at the minority of Aunare who despised me or maybe anger at himself for not taking a stronger position against his weak, war-fearing advisors. But it very well might be aimed at me.

If that was the case, I'd deal with it. Just not right now.

One thing at a time. I would get through the rest of the interview, and then I hoped I could salvage my relationship with Lorne.

Either way, saving my heart wasn't worth the lives of so many innocents. This was more important. So, I pushed my worry about Lorne's anger away.

"When this is over, if the Aunare still think the same thing—that I'm not fit to rule, that there should be no war, that Space-Tech should be allowed to destroy the Aunare—then I guess I'll have some difficult choices to make. Because I won't sit here and do nothing. I *can't*. But I also won't rule a people that hate me so much. I won't sit here and take the attention from where it's needed. Because while the reporters are busy digging into my life, my past, my future, they're ignoring the bigger truth about the Aunare and the danger that we are in."

The Aunare had believed SpaceTech's lies for too long. I had to make them see the evil that they were dealing with and hopefully show them that I wasn't their enemy.

This interview was the only way I could do that. It was the one time I had everyone's attention live. Which meant that the media wouldn't be able to mutilate my message through short, quippy clips.

So, I was taking over this interview.

It was my platform now.

CHAPTER FIFTEEN

AMIHANNA

THERE WAS nothing but the crackles and pops from the fire to break the silence. I'd probably insulted all of them by calling them lazy and cowards—not in so many words, but that was the gist. No one knew what to say to that. Not even Himani. He sat across from me with his eyes wide, and as he watched me, I could almost see questions starting to form, but his lips stayed still, silent, waiting.

And that was okay. Himani didn't need to ask me anything because I had plenty more to say.

I could feel Lorne still tense beside me, and I knew the only way I could get through this was to push him out of my mind. He was a distraction, and I couldn't afford to worry about hurting his feelings. Not right now.

"Roan?" I held up three fingers to my best friend, and he threw a thumbnail-size disc at me. I caught it, scooted the water cups on the coffee table over, and placed the disc on the table between us. One of the cameras hovering in the room moved closer to get a good shot of what I'd put on the table.

"That's a holo disc. Do you know what she's going to play for us?" Himani asked Lorne.

"No." Lorne leaned toward the table. "But she has my attention."

"And mine," Himani muttered as he scooted his chair forward.

I didn't plan to play this one first, but I hadn't known that Himani would start his interview asking me about what happened in the Sel'Ani arena. But I could be flexible in my plans, and this would transition smoothly into what I needed to talk about.

I tapped the disc, and a holographic image popped up, enlarging until it took up a third of the coffee table, becoming a 3D vid of a seventeen-year-old boy being dragged into a crowded Earther arena, where all were cheering for his death.

Lorne gripped my hand as the boy's skin lit up, showing his *fao'ana* bright along his skin. The boy was crying and begging for his life, until they released the dogs. And then the boy started to move, running, screaming for someone to help him, for someone to save him.

But no one came for him. No one would save him.

Lorne's skin started to flash. I squeezed his hand and concentrated on our frequencies—not knowing if I could just will them to balance him out—but he got it under control. I was thankful that he was able to hang in because this was going to get worse. A lot worse.

When the first dog ripped into the halfer's flesh, I turned the volume down. "I don't know if you remember, but I brought this up in the Sel'Ani arena. This is the specific boy from the day Declan found me."

"I remember everything you said that day." Lorne's voice was firm and clear, yet it sounded like he wasn't even fully thinking about what he said. It made me curious, but I didn't dare look at him.

Himani jerked in his leather armchair as one of the dogs went for the boy's neck and the light in the boy's skin went out. "This is worse than I imagined. I can't... Can you..." Himani covered his eyes for a second before pulling his shaking hand away to look at me.

"It's really hard to watch." I tapped the screen, cutting off the sound of the Earthers yelling for more blood. For another to be thrown into the arena. Because one dead halfer wasn't enough. "I've seen this kind of thing a lot, and it's still hard."

"This is horrific," Lorne said. "I don't have words. Is this a yearly event? Do they execute someone on the anniversary of our split every single year?"

Before I could try to answer, the feed cut off, transitioning to very short clips—flashes really—of thousands of faces. Aunare and halfer. Children and adults. Male and female. Some with glowing skin and some without. All moments before their deaths in the arena. Roan didn't find all of them, but he found enough to get the point across.

"I think that last part answered your question, Lorne. But in case it didn't, these executions aren't once a year, one person kind of a thing. It doesn't happen as often anymore because there aren't very many of us alive on Earth or the colonies. Those of us that made it through Liberation Week—and the thirteen years after—survived by being extremely good at hiding. But yes. It happened a lot. When they first introduced the execution arena, it went on for hours every day, for weeks on end. It slowed after that to a few times a week, and it's slowed even more in the years since this started. SpaceTech sees it now as an as-needed type of thing. But it's still happening. It never stopped."

The holographic vid hit the end and turned off, but the room was so quiet that I wasn't sure anyone was breathing anymore. The Aunare were all staring at the spot where the holograph was just moments before. Their gazes frozen to the spot. The only thing that made noise was the cameras as they moved to take in everyone in the room.

I'd been expecting questions at this point, but that was okay. It was a lot to process, and I had a lot more to show them.

"A few years ago, SpaceTech started throwing Earthers into the arena, too. Anyone they consider traitor is fair game, even if no evidence was released to prove every person they executed was an actual traitor. It's become a way to control their people with fear." I was quiet for a moment to give everyone some time. Slowly, everyone in the room moved to look at me. One of the cameras buzzed closer, and I did my best to ignore it.

"This is why I said I couldn't watch someone else die in an arena. This is the kind of enemy we're dealing with. This is SpaceTech, and they hate us." I had their attention now, and I hoped that the Aunare who were watching the live feed were also paying attention.

And now we were back to where I wanted to start.

I let go of Lorne's hand to hold up one finger to Roan, and he tossed me another disc.

"This is a compilation of Earther newsreel footage from Liberation Week. I don't know how much was seen here, and it feels like every time I bring up how bad it was, the Aunare are shocked. So, before I decide that you've lost my complete respect, I thought I should make some facts very clear. If you weren't previously aware of what was happening on Earth and its colonies, you will learn it now. The Aunare cannot afford to be ignorant any longer." I scooted the disc with the arena footage to the side and placed the next disc down. I caught a look that wasn't quite disgust and wasn't quite horror from Himani. I didn't know him, so I wasn't sure what to make of it.

"Are you okay, Himani?"

"No. And I don't know that I ever will be again." His voice shook and his skin had turned a little green.

I grabbed one of the glasses of water from the coffee table and handed it to him.

"Thank you," he said after he took a drink. "I've never seen anything so horrific in my life, and I covered the battles in the outer reaches in my first years of reporting. I wasn't prepared to witness something like that today."

I almost felt like I should warn him about what was coming next. The executions weren't the worst of it. Not even close. But I didn't say anything because I needed everyone to see him and Lorne experiencing this footage. I needed everyone watching the live feed to understand what we were up against.

We'd come to a point where it was fight the war or surrender to SpaceTech, and I needed them to choose to fight. I needed them to stop their crusade against me and finally see what they were up against.

I looked straight into the camera hovering in front of me. "For the next vid, I tried my best to pick some moments that are indicative of what happened to the Aunare people across Earth and its colonies during Liberation Week." It had been horrible to weed through all the footage, but this was more important than sparing myself from the nightmares it had given me. "As with the Earther execution arena footage, this shouldn't be easy for you to watch, but that makes it more important that you pay attention. Please, honor the lives that were lost by watching. Today, the Aunare are resisting war against SpaceTech. It is my hope that after I'm done with this interview, you'll wonder why anyone was ever against taking down SpaceTech."

I tapped the disc, and it started playing without sound. Roan and I decided that having sound on this one made it unwatchable. It was too horrific. As I watched Himani's face, I knew that was the right call. I spared a quick glance at Lorne, but his kingly mask was in place. I couldn't read him. Not really. Not by any visible cue.

I focused back on the vid that showed an Earther street. Roan and I had been scanning footage for days, prepping for my takeover of this interview. I couldn't believe our luck when we found this particular clip.

A group of Aunare were running down a street chased by Earthers, but when they reached the end of the street, they would only find more Earthers waiting to kill them. There was no escape.

A few of the Aunare hit the pavement, dying in front of the camera. Their bodies lying on the ground—breathing their last breaths—as others trampled them, trying to get away. But they wouldn't.

They wouldn't.

But that wasn't the most essential part of this clip.

I would've missed the important part entirely if I hadn't recognized the faces of the dead Aunare. I could still smell their blood, hear their screams, feel their deaths in the air. I wanted to scream with them, but I couldn't. I couldn't scream then, and I wouldn't scream now.

Just watching the clip again made me feel panicked. I was back there on the street. Ready to run, run, run for my life.

But I was in a room. A safe room on Sel'Ani, so far away from that street on Earth. I wanted to reach out for Lorne's hand again, but it felt too selfish of me to take comfort from him when I was forcing him to watch.

The recording zoomed in on two figures huddled behind a dumpster, and I paused it. The figures were grainy and just a little pixilated. Their faces couldn't be seen, but I knew who they were. Everyone else would just have to take my word for it.

"That's me." My voice cracked, and it was as if the silence that had frozen everyone in the room suddenly shattered.

There were gasps and a few people cried out as everyone in the room looked at me.

There was a rising hum and flickering from Lorne, but I trusted him enough not to totally lose it. And I didn't trust myself to look at him and not break. Because watching this footage was hard. Not just for everyone else, but for me, too.

I glanced across the room. "And the figure beside me is my mother," I said as I watched a tear roll down her cheek.

One of the cameras whirled toward my mother, and she brushed at the tear quickly, trying to hide it from view. "That's us." Her gaze moved to me. "It was awful—a nightmare that I thought we couldn't survive. I had so little hope that day, but I was alone with my baby. My innocent little girl. I had to keep trying. I had to keep going. For you, I kept moving even when I thought we wouldn't live to take one more step." She tried to smile but failed. Mom always liked to brush over anything unpleasant, but even she knew there wasn't a way to downplay this. Not when it was there for everyone to witness.

"We survived. By luck or fate or... maybe it was just chance." Mom shrugged because there wasn't a reason why we lived when others didn't. "But we made it through that day."

"We did, but too many weren't as lucky as us." I hit play again, and the footage showed me jumping into the dumpster and my mother jumping in after me. She reached up, closing us inside the dumpster. The video zoomed out and panned away, following the fleeing Aunare, but I paused before the dumpster's image was gone.

"We hid in there all day, all night, and the whole next day, too. It wasn't my only time hiding in a dumpster, but it was the first and definitely the most terrifying. We were too scared to make a sound because this is what was going on around us."

I hit play again.

The image continued to pan, showing what was happening to the rest of the Aunare at the end of the street.

A lot of the Earthers didn't have guns, but they had bats and bits of metal and anything they could find. They were beating the Aunare until they were piles of meat and bones.

Not all Aunare were like me. Not all of them came from a line like the di Aetes—a bloodline of warriors. The average Aunare might be a little faster than humans, a little stronger, but not enough to withstand a mob of that size.

No one could stand against the Earthers that day. Not even my guards. They'd sacrificed themselves to give me and my mother a chance to run. For a long time, I tried not to think about them and their sacrifice, even though I'd been grateful for it. It was too hard. But now, I stared at my new guards, and I promised myself that such a sacrifice would never be needed again.

Never again.

But Eshrin—my head guard—was watching me. He pressed his fist to his heart and bowed his head, and I knew given the same choice as my childhood guards, he'd give his life for mine. *Not happening. Not ever again.*

I forced myself to look away from Eshrin. Many of the others in the room began to close their eyes, unable to watch the horror of so many violently dying.

But even if they couldn't watch, I knew that they understood. I glanced back at the footage and hit pause.

"I'm confused," Himani said. "These all look like non-Space-Tech Earthers attacking the Aunare. Where was SpaceTech?"

"If you remember back then, you'll know there was a lot of tension between Earthers and the Aunare."

"I do. If I'm remembering accurately, I believe there was news that the Aunare were thinking about pulling out of any SpaceTech controlled territory."

"Yes. Exactly. You see, this wasn't something that just happened overnight. SpaceTech had been working for years to seed hatred for the Aunare among the Earthers. By the time Liberation Week started, they'd already convinced the Earthers that the Aunare were the enemy. That you were the reason that their life was spent begging for scraps and living like slaves to the corporation. It was all lies, but they believed it." This would be difficult to explain. I needed them to not be angry with the Earthers. They weren't the ones to blame for all of this. "Although there was something that set these mobs off."

"What happened?"

"Bombs. It was the bombs that sent the Earthers into a frenzy."

"What bombs?" Lorne asked. "What did SpaceTech do that day?"

"You don't know?" I don't know why I was always surprised

when everything about Liberation Week was a mystery to him, but it still surprised me. How could he not know? How could the Aunare not know this?

And that's exactly why I was doing this now. Because they were blaming me for everything, they were focused on me. They couldn't afford to do that anymore. Those lies that kept me labeled as the problem were just part of SpaceTech's plan. I was going to make them *see* the truth.

"No. All we know is we lost contact. We didn't know what happened until Rysden got there, and by then, it was too late."

"Liberation Week began when bombs started going off around major Earth and colony cities. SpaceTech said it was the Aunare that did it. You were attacking us. They said that we were now at war, and Earthers should kill all Aunare on sight. So all the Earthers took to the streets with whatever weapons they had. They went after their friends and neighbors. They marched down the streets, dragging them out of their beds to kill them."

"We didn't set off any bombs," my father said. "We knew how tense it was. We were doing our best to ease that tension. There was no way we would've done that. Not even the former King would've allowed that." He sounded defensive, but he didn't need to be.

"I know you didn't. Especially since one of the bombs destroyed our house."

"What?" Lorne's question was soft, but I felt like it was a lie.

I couldn't detect any hum or a flicker or anything, but my gut told me to grip his hand. I hoped that would help enough with his anger while I looked at my father. "It was a good thing Mom and I were sleeping in the basement that night. If we hadn't..." I sighed. "Some of the bombs were in the Aunare quadrants of the cities, but most of them were in Earther areas—in their apartment buildings and markets. They were all set by SpaceTech to inflame mobs. To make anyone who might see through their charade too angry to think clearly anymore. To make everyone believe the Aunare had attacked *first*, and now they were the sworn enemy. All Aunare had to die."

My father stared down at the ground for a moment and I watched him as his hands tightened into fists and then loosened. Fists, loose. Fists, loose. As if he were trying to will away his anger.

If it worked, I might have to try that technique, but from the hunch of his shoulders, I was pretty sure it wasn't working at all.

I focused back on Himani. "When the Earther media said it was the Aunare who were bombing every major city on Earth and its colonies, the Earthers believed the media without questioning any of their information. They kept pushing out onto every media channel they could find these little clips of mothers crying over their dead babies or little kids being pulled from rubble, and when that wasn't moving things along enough, they played the clips on the sides of buildings and on billboards. No one got a break from the manipulation. Not even for a moment. It was a constant bombardment, and it was enough to make anyone angry enough to act without thinking. No one with a soul could stand by when their children were being hurt."

It seemed like such a blatant manipulation, but I understood why the Earthers believed the lies. "The corporation had been campaigning against the Aunare for *years*. So, of course the Earthers bought the media's lies as truth, and they reacted with violence."

I motioned to the frozen footage on the table. "There were rats in the dumpster and it stank and we had no water, but we stayed silently inside because otherwise, we would've ended up just like the rest of the Aunare on Earth." I hit play again.

The footage moved to scene after scene of Aunare and halfers being hunted down and killed. One after another. City after city. Planet after planet. I let it keep playing though it was already too much, even for me. Even though I'd seen it before. Even though I'd lived it before.

The panic to run, hide, survive was beating in my veins, but I was safe.

And still, a drip of cold sweat ran down my spine. My hand shook as I reached for my glass of water on the table. I almost didn't grab the water, but I needed it. Shaking hands wasn't as bad as throwing up on live, intergalactic feeds.

I downed half the glass and set it back on the table. No one said a word as the footage continued to play.

Before the interview started, the room had been animated with questions and excitement and setting up for what was going to happen. Now I could only feel the horror in the room. It was a thick, suffocating blanket, and even I couldn't take it anymore.

I tapped the disc, turning off the vid, but still, no one made a noise.

There was nothing to say.

I gestured with two fingers, and Roan threw another disc at me. I was thankful when my shaking hands caught it. "The slaughter of Aunare on SpaceTech controlled planets has been going on for years. What I just played was only the beginning. It never stopped." That was something that the Aunare on Sel'Ani needed to understand.

I hit play with no sound again. "This is from about five years ago. It started on one of the colony planets when they found a pocket of hidden Aunare, but once others realized that there might be more hiding, the hunt for Aunare eventually spread to a few other colonies."

This disc was eerily similar to the last—Aunare being killed in the streets, in their homes, in the places they'd been hiding, hoping no one would find them. But they did. So many were found and killed.

In some of the footage, major landmarks were visible, which told everyone in the room just how widespread the slaughter was. It was everywhere, and yet, the Aunare had done nothing.

I couldn't watch the vid, even without sound. My stomach—

my heart—couldn't take reliving it again. Five years ago, I'd been obsessed with watching every scrap of footage I could find —both SpaceTech and off the grid—and all it did was make me angry, depressed, and full of hopelessness. After days in bed, I let Roan drag me from to the warehouse gym. It took me a long time to come back from that dark pit of despair.

Going back to that time in my life wouldn't help me at all. Instead, I watched everyone else in the room. My mother was staring at the ground. She couldn't watch it either. We'd seen it before, and it had been hard enough then.

My father's skin was glowing as he watched beside her, which meant he was upset, but I couldn't figure out what he was thinking. His face wasn't giving anything away, and I didn't know him well enough to notice any of his tells.

There was a tic in Roan's jaw. I knew he wanted to turn this off. He hated watching any footage of the slaughter, but he hated it because he saw me in every Aunare being killed. The last week of compiling footage had really taken a toll on him. There were shadows under his eyes, and his quick draw smile had disappeared. I hated that I'd put him through this, but it was my best plan.

Fynea stood with her spine rigid and eyes wide, but I didn't know what she was thinking either. She was Lorne's best friend. We'd trained together some, but we didn't know each other that well yet. Not enough to click.

The rest of the assistants and security seemed to have some of the same emotions. Some of them were crying. Some of them looked like they were ready to fight. All of them were unable to hide their anger, sadness, and heartbreak. All of them were glowing. I'd never been in a room with so many glowing people, and I wasn't sure how I felt about it, except that I noticed none of them were ashamed of it or trying to hide what they felt. I hoped one day I could be able to feel the same confidence in my skin as they did.

I looked at Lorne last. His face was still a mask like my

father's, but I knew him. Or maybe it was that I was his *shalshasa* and could see through the facade he put up.

Lorne was angry. It didn't matter how I knew, I just knew it.

The vid went dark and turned off, and then I held up four fingers.

The motion caught Lorne's attention. "For the love of the Goddess, how many discs do you have?" Lorne squeezed his eyes shut. "Please. No more. I can't take it."

"Just one more, and you've seen it before." I gripped his hand and hit play. "*Everyone* has seen this one. I'm only playing it because after surviving all of this, not to mention Abaddon—which everyone has seen by now—this is the welcoming I got when I came home."

I hit play, and it showed a compilation of their news reports about me from after I saved their capital city and their king. There was a brief moment of footage when the media seemed to get behind me. Lorne had freed them from his father's control and they were allowed to finally report freely. But then slowly, it got worse again. They were discussing assassination attempts—debating if I deserved them—and then turned into anger that I was causing a war by being back on Sel'Ani, and then twisted into the outright hatred that I'd been allowed to keep my betrothal to Lorne. Opinion pieces and gossip got more and more screen time, which made it nearly impossible for anything of substance to be reported, let alone anything that was anti-SpaceTech or even slightly pro-war.

I was a distraction the Aunare couldn't afford.

I leaned back against the loveseat and watched the short video. It didn't need to be very long to get my point across. Every Aunare knew what was on there. This was something they'd lived through, but it would serve as a reminder of what they'd said and done in the last couple of weeks.

When the last disc turned off, Lorne and Himani looked up at me.

Himani's face wasn't so green anymore, but he looked like

he'd just aged an eon. Deep lines shadowed his face around his mouth. It was awful to be a part of hurting anyone like that, but it wasn't Himani's expression that slayed me. It was Lorne's.

I had a second to be worried for him before he ripped off his crown and threw it high into the air. He screamed and it was a sound that tore into my heart.

I had a second of confusion and then there was a small pop as it broke into embers, but what rained down was cold ash.

He'd destroyed his crown.

Oh God. Lorne had destroyed his crown on a live intergalactic feed.

Every other person in the room instantly dropped to one knee, bowing their heads, fist pressed to their hearts.

He bowed his head, fingers in his hair, and I knew—I *knew* without any reason that I should know—that Lorne was about to lose control.

I had to do something. I'd hurt him, and I couldn't fix it. I couldn't change what I'd done or how I'd done it. I just hoped it was worth the pain I'd caused.

I twisted on the loveseat so that I could hold him, tugging him toward me. "It's okay."

He dropped his forehead to my shoulder. "No. It's really not. This is my fault. I should've taken the throne years ago. I should've forced it. I should've—"

"Stop it."

"All those lives. They're on my head. All of—"

I pushed him away. "No." I said the word loudly, firmly, because he had to hear me. "No. That's not why I did this. I wanted you to see. I wanted everyone to see. But the time to blame and look back at the past is done. It's gone. We don't have time for it. Suck it up, Lorne."

He looked up at me and the pain in his face, in his soul, it was so acute it took my breath away.

I prayed for courage to finish this and finish it well.

I stood up and picked up all the discs from the table.

"This is the past. It's over. We can't change any of it." I threw them into the air, and then shoved my hand at them, using my power to destroy them in one move. "It's done," I screamed.

I took a few deep breaths, and then when I was calmer, I spoke again. "But I want to leave everyone with not only the truth about what happened, but with *hope*. We can't change the past, but we can let it inform our decisions. So, what are we going to do now? Where do we go from here? That's worth talking about."

I moved back to sit on the couch next to Lorne. He was trying to gain control again, and I gave him my hand. "SpaceTech is drawing closer. They've got ships too close to our space, to our colonies, and if you're not very, very careful, it's going to be you hiding in a dumpster, running for your life, while SpaceTech slaughters everyone you love on your home planet."

"You can't allow this!" One of Himani's people yelled from behind the camera-control bank. I caught the man with his hand over his mouth, as if he couldn't believe the words he'd said.

"I'm not allowing anything. I'm here training for war. I'm ready to fight. I'm ready to die to stop this war. But what I'm hearing from the Aunare, what's being reported, and all the attempts on my life, *you* are going to allow this to happen. The Aunare have a choice to make. You can either keep going down the dangerous path you are already on and lose the war. Or you can get up. Stand up. Do your part in taking down SpaceTech. I chose the second path. What do you choose?"

I hoped that they would be with me, but no matter what, Lorne and I would do what needed to be done.

CHAPTER SIXTEEN

AMIHANNA

HIMANI RECOVERED the fastest of anyone in the room. "Rumblings came through, but we all collectively ignored them." Himani's voice was soft and thready. "We didn't want to believe anything bad was happening. So, we believed what was easiest." His gaze was full of unshed tears as he finally looked up at me again. "I was angry when you said we were lazy and selfish earlier, but now I see your point. I can understand now. And it's a horrible truth to face." He leaned back in the armchair. "This has been hard to watch. I think I'll need a few days to fully process not just what I've seen, but my role as a member of the media in letting these atrocities happen."

There was a relief that came to me with Himani's words. I'd gotten through to him, which meant that I had to have gotten through to at least some of the Aunare. I couldn't change what happened in the past, but I could change the path that the Aunare were on. I could make a difference to the Aunare and innocent Earthers that were still fighting against SpaceTech.

So that's what I had to try to do. "I'm sorry for—"

"No, child. Do not apologize. Not ever. Not when it is we who owe you the greatest of apologies."

The room was quiet, and for the first time today, I wasn't sure what to say next. Except for one thing. "We need to be united against SpaceTech. We can't afford to sit back and let SpaceTech take any more from the Aunare than they already have."

"I have a question. If I may?" Himani's shoulders were a little slouched, and the lines on his face seemed deeper. It was like the information I'd shared had been a physical weight to him.

He was definitely going to need more than a few days to process everything.

I gave him a small nod. "Of course." I'd honestly expected a lot more questions from him throughout the footage.

"The train cars in Albuquerque. You mentioned them to me in the arena." Himani tilted his head as he stared at me.

"What's the question?" If he'd asked one, I hadn't heard it.

"Are there really train cars of Aunare bones on Earth?"

He had to be kidding. "Why would I make up something like that?"

"It's true. All of it," Roan said from behind the cameras.

Himani nodded slowly. "You're right. We can't sit here and do nothing. Not anymore." Himani's skin lit from within. "Not anymore."

Finally. This. This is what I needed to hear. Someone who was on the same page as I was. "I know you're angry right now. I know this was hard. I promise you it was so much harder living through all of that than it was to watch it. That anger that you're feeling right now after watching all those people die? That's raging even hotter inside me. It's had thirteen years to burn. So, when your news reporters call me angry or grumpy, please remember what you're feeling right now."

I hoped that everyone watching the feed right now was feeling the same things as those in the room with me now. "I'm not your enemy. I will fight to protect the Aunare with everything that I am. I will fight until I have no more air in my lungs, and then I will fight some more. And if I can ask one more question of you—ask yourself why anyone would speak out against me? If I'm here to protect you, what are the Aunare that hate me truly doing? Because it's not anything good."

"You've given us so much to think on, and I'm thankful that we have a leader in charge that will save us despite our faults. I —" Himani's voice shook. "I think I need to pause the live feed now," Himani said into the camera in front of him. "But I have a few parting words before I sign off."

He stared down at his lap for a second, and then looked back again, straight into the camera. This time, the broken look was a little less. He'd put it away to give them a clear message, and I hoped it was good.

"Amihanna di Aetes has lived up to her lineage and done it proud. She's given all of us a lot to think about." The shaking was gone from Himani's voice. "I don't want to waste any of your time while I struggle with what I now see is the truth, but I know that—without any doubt in my soul—that we, the Aunare people, have hard work to do. Every single Aunare alive has work to do." He paused for a moment. "My work means that I endeavor to find answers to why this was such a shock to me. I'm a person of the media, and I should have known. It's my job to keep all of you informed, and I failed at that. I need to know why we lied to you so horribly, and who exactly is behind all these evil stories on an innocent young woman who might become the greatest leader the Aunare have ever seen." His voice got shaky again, and he took a moment to gather himself. "I'll have more of my report before the evening news. Watch for alerts from my channel with updates. And until then, I will say, we all owe our life and our support to Amihanna di Aetes. If for nothing else than for making us see. We owe her a debt, and I— for one—will work my hardest to repay it. She has my full support as our future High Queen."

I'd hoped he would leave them with a good final message, but this was better than good. This was amazing, and way more than I dreamed I'd get from him.

Now I had a strong vote in my favor from a man who had a

massive following with the Aunare. If I'd changed his mind, then I had to have gotten through to at least some of the audience watching.

The cameras all zoomed back to Himani's crew, and I let out a long breath.

Done.

I'd made it through. I wanted to run from the room and from everyone watching me, but I forced myself to move slowly as I stood.

I wanted to look at Lorne, but I wasn't sure what he was thinking or feeling and I was terrified that by not giving him a warning, I'd broken something with us.

He'd destroyed his crown. On a live feed.

He was sitting there with his head bowed, forearms on his knees, and he looked like a broken king.

I'd broken him.

I assumed he needed a minute. I hoped after that he'd want to talk to me.

So, I was a coward as I rose from my spot and prayed that I could slip out of the room without notice.

The other people in the room were talking softly to each other. I gave a nod to Himani and moved to leave, but my father crossed the room quickly, gripping my wrist before I could get to the door.

I stopped and turned back to him. He looked heartbroken, but it wasn't from the footage I'd played or the truths I'd spoken. It was his job to know what happened on Earth, and he'd been back to Earth before. He knew what it was like. So, why did he look like his soul had just been ripped from his body?

"What?"

"You really slept in that dumpster?"

Seriously? After everything I'd shown him today that was what he was focused on?

I glanced at Mom. Sometimes I didn't think we were alike at all, and then she said or did something, and it was so clear that I was her kid. I held back from Lorne just as much as she held back from my father. "You haven't told him?"

Mom gave me this little sigh, and I knew what she was going to say. I knew it, but I needed to hear it. She'd been distant ever since I got here, and she seemed to be over everything. Like it never happened, and when I couldn't snap my fingers and be done with the past, she left me to struggle alone.

My father abandoned me on Earth thirteen years ago, and my mother abandoned me when we got to Sel'Ani weeks ago.

She wrung her fingers together. "It was hard coming back here, *mija*." She was quiet for a second before continuing. "You know how I am. I don't talk about my emotions much, and I was grateful to finally be safe and with your father again. It didn't seem like it would do any good to talk about it. And so I didn't. I just wanted it to be over, so..."

So she left me to deal with the trauma on my own. "And now?"

Mom walked across the room and wrapped her arms around me. "And now, I know I can't ignore the pain of the past. Especially when my daughter is brave enough to face it straight on." She turned to my father but kept her arms around me. "We survived, but barely. *Barely.* She wasn't brushing over the bad parts on that arena stage, but she didn't go into any details. She showed some of it today, but that dumpster part was just a moment really. One moment in thirteen years of struggling every single day. It was worse and harder than anything she's said. It was worse being there than it was to watch it. I promise you that."

She squeezed me tighter before letting me go. "It was hard for me these last thirteen years, but so much worse for her because she protected me so many times. If I got caught, I would be okay. But she was from a strong bloodline. There was no hiding what she was, and yet, she was so brave and strong. A true di Aetes. She worked, she saved to buy a ship, she made plan after plan of how to escape, she taught kids to defend themselves, she patrolled the streets to keep us and our neighbors safe, and she never gave up. She—"

"Mom." She was making me out to be a saint, and I wasn't. I really wasn't. Especially not after what I'd done today. "We *both* worked hard to survive."

She laughed. "No. Not like you did. And after years on the run, we eventually found a home. It wasn't much, but it was mostly safe." She reached a hand out, and Roan stepped toward her. "And most importantly, we had friends who became family. Who protected us."

"Damn right you did," Roan said. "The Crew had your back."

I gave my mom a kiss on the cheek. The tiny cameras zoomed around us to get the action from multiple angles. I'd thought that when the cameras went back to their crew, that the live-feed *and* the recording had stopped. Apparently not.

I did my best to see past the cameras when I looked at Roan and motioned toward the door.

"I was hoping for a few follow-up questions." Himani called out to me. "I've ended the live feed to give the audience—and myself—time to breathe. I think we all need it, but I feel like if I let you go now, I'll never get to talk to you again. I know you don't love giving interviews, but... I need a moment to compose myself, then I'd like to talk again. In an hour or so? If you'll allow it."

"I have to train." I paused for a second. He'd signed off, and I thought we were done. But he was right. I wasn't planning on doing another interview. Hopefully not for a while. I felt exposed enough as it was, but I wasn't sure what to do.

"You were listening a few minutes ago, right?" I asked Himani. "You did hear the part about the ongoing war? About how we need to be ready, which means I should be spending every second I have preparing. I don't know when I'll have time for another interview like this."

"Oh, I heard every word you spoke, but I'd love a little more of your time. Given everything you've shown me, I think I finally have a few questions. I need a moment to get my thoughts together and talk to my crew. Do a little research. Might I join you while you train? By the time you're finished, I should be ready. I could ask you some things when you're done. I'm happy to wait. It won't be live, and I'll show all of your people what I plan to use before airing."

I wasn't sure what to do, and no one seemed to be stepping in for me—so I dared a look back at Lorne. He was still sitting on the loveseat. His mask was in place as he watched me, and I desperately wanted to be alone with him.

Later. We'd talk later. And if he was upset with me, I would deal with that then.

I looked at Himani and then back at Lorne, hoping he'd understand my question.

He gave me a small shrug as if to tell me that this was my show. He was hiding something, but I wasn't sure what. Other than anger. At me? At the past? I wasn't sure.

I wanted to be done with Himani and this interview. I wanted to talk to Lorne. I wanted to take a minute to push the past back where it belonged. But I was okay with Himani coming to my training session. It might even be good if he came with his cameras.

"It wouldn't be live?"

"No."

"And if I want something cut?"

"Roan has been very outspoken about what's allowed. He can work with my assistants to have anything sensitive either cut or important details blurred or skipped over."

It seemed fair, but I wasn't sure if extending the interview and letting him follow me to my training session was a good idea. His cameras were still following us, and I wondered if he ever really turned them off.

Screw it. This interview was supposed to be for the Aunare to learn more about me. What better way than if they saw me train?

"Sure, follow me. You can ask questions as I take breaks in my training. Any footage to be released needs to be approved by Roan. Okay?"

"That's very fair of you and much appreciated," he said, rising from his chair, sending his assistants and production people scrambling to grab everything they needed from the room.

I nodded to Eshrin, who was standing by the door. I knew he'd follow me as I stepped into the hallway with Roan. Two of my guards stepped away from where they were leaning against the wall outside the interview room and started moving down the hallway, clearing the path for me.

The hallways were usually mostly empty, but today it was filled with guards, housemaids tidying up after the crew, kitchen staff making sure the narrow tables they'd lined the halls with were stocked with snacks and beverages, and then all the crew and everyone who had piled in the room to watch the filming that were now leaving. It added up to a lot of people in one hallway.

My guards knew where I was going next, even though they had to adjust the plan to include a crowd of observers. Eshrin was tapping on his wrist unit, and I knew he was most likely signaling for backup.

Oh man. This was going to turn into a circus, and I was already regretting inviting Himani to join us.

I peeked over my shoulder. Himani was a few feet behind me, whispering with one of his slew of assistants. My parents were beside him. My guards were mixed with Lorne's and spread throughout the group. The little flying cameras started moving through the hallway, trying to keep up with me as they filmed. But Lorne still stood back in the doorway to the informal meeting room. He was leaning close to Fynea, whispering in her ear, probably so that he wouldn't be overheard.

I faced forward and kept walking, but a second later, I looked back, and Lorne was weaving his way through the people to get to me.

He wrapped an arm around me as soon as he was close enough. "You could've warned me," his lips brushed my ear as he whispered.

I put a hand over my mouth to hide my lips from the cameras and whispered back to him. "I could've—and I almost did—but I wanted your reaction to be honest. I didn't want there to be any arguments that I had staged some big production to manipulate the Aunare and that you were somehow complicit in it."

CHAPTER SEVENTEEN

AMIHANNA

WE REACHED the gym before Himani could ask any more questions, which was good. I needed a break as much as he did. Especially after Lorne's freak-out.

I pushed through the gym doors and already felt more at ease. Gyms had always been my home away from home, and this one was by far the best I'd ever used.

I wanted to change clothes, but now that Himani and his crew were following me, I didn't exactly have time for that. The pants Almya had put me in were actually really stretchy. I could train in them no problem, but I hoped the blouse held up. It was basically a halter tank. I was pretty sure it'd stay where it was supposed to—the built-in support halter bra was tight enough to keep me covered—but I wasn't sure if I'd end up ripping the outer, more silky shell.

Oh well. I guessed if I ripped it, Almya would just have to fix it.

I motioned to the benches. "You and your crew can have a seat," I said to Himani. "As I said before, you're welcome to stay, film, and ask questions when I have a break." He started to speak, and I held up a finger. "I may or may not answer them, but you can always ask. Mostly, I hope you'll watch, listen, and learn what I am, who I am, and what I'm doing to play my part in the war against SpaceTech. Roan will stay with you to approve all the footage you keep."

I knew Himani already had a question for me, but I needed more time. I kept walking past the stands that were nearly full with Aunare. The first few mornings that Lorne and I trained in here, we didn't have any visitors watching, but slowly over the last few days, as everyone on the estate started to learn our schedule, more and more people showed up.

Now, it seemed that whenever I was in here, the stands were full, but it didn't bother me, at least not very much. As long as Lorne was here, I was okay. Everything else faded a little.

But in the afternoons, there were times that I made Eshrin ask people to leave. Sometimes I just wanted to let go and not worry about what people would think.

Today, I was going to have a crowd, and that was okay. At least I wasn't on a live feed anymore.

The magical gym floor softened as I sat down to stretch. I loved this gym so much, but the floor was my second love—Lorne was my first love. It gave me the confidence to try out new moves and push myself harder than I've ever pushed myself before. It was next level frost.

Lorne sat heavily on the floor next to me, but instead of stretching, he just stared at me.

This wasn't good. I looked around for the cameras, but they were hanging back by Himani. I didn't think they were close enough to get any of our actual words if they couldn't see my lips. I bent over one leg. "Are you okay?"

"No." Lorne moved to sit in front of me, putting his back to the cameras. "That didn't go as I thought it would," he said softly. "I'm sorry I got so upset after."

"I'm sorry I took you by surprise."

He shrugged.

"Are you mad?" He didn't seem mad. His skin wasn't flickering anymore, and I couldn't feel any shifts in his frequency, but that didn't mean that he wasn't upset with me. He was much more experienced in shielding his frequencies and moods.

I spun my engagement ring around my finger with my thumb as I straightened. He wasn't angry enough to ask for it back. I was sure of that much.

"No, but I feel like I owe you an apology."

He owed me an apology after what I'd just pulled? "Why?"

"I just…" He took a long slow breath. Six. Then out three.

If he was still this out of control, then I knew I'd really hurt him. It was tearing me apart to see him like this and to know it was my fault. I wasn't sure how to make it up to him. "Lorne—"

"The footage upset me."

He would've had to be missing his soul for what I'd shown not to upset him. "I can tell. Is there anything you want to talk to me about specifically? Maybe if we talk about it, you'll feel better." I needed more information about what was really setting him off the most if I was going to help him calm down.

His eyes went a little glassy as he stared off at nothing. "Everything. All of it." He shook his head and met my gaze. "You in a dumpster. You—the innocent, sweet Amihanna I used to know and love, who used to go through the door in our closet when she had a nightmare, who I swore to protect, crawling into a dumpster. That took my breath away and I can't… I can't seem to catch it."

It was strange to me that the dumpster was the worst for him, but it really wasn't the worst thing I played on those discs. It was only bad because it was me—the me he remembered from before—and he'd loved me.

It was weird how both he and my father found that clip the hardest to watch. All that death and horror I played, but it was me in a dumpster that got to them.

"That's not the worst of where I lived, Lorne. I was really only in there for a day. It was a blip. I mean, being on Earth after Liberation Week was awful, especially those first few years."

He closed his eyes. "You're making it worse." He started taking measured breaths again.

There was nothing I could say that could change the truth of what happened that day. It'd been awful. I tried to search my mind for anything positive about that dumpster, but there was nothing positive. No lesson I learned that was good. Nothing.

I tried to come up with something to explain how I was okay now, but he didn't agree with that. I wasn't sure how to help him other than shutting up, but I had to do something.

I leaned forward and brushed a kiss against his forehead, and said the only thing I thought might help. "I love you."

His glow brightened, and I wasn't sure if I'd just made it worse again.

Damn it. I should've shut up.

I went back to stretching, as if by going on, I'd will his frequencies to settle and balance. I pulled my arm across my chest and leaned into my shoulder.

My parents came to stand in front of me, and I stopped stretching to look up at my mother. "Am I in trouble?" Because she had that look on her face.

"No, but I feel like I owe you an apology," Mom said.

There was no stopping my laugh. "What? Why in the wide universe of crazy would you ever need to apologize to me?"

"Because I've been ignoring what we went through."

Oh. That.

Okay. That was fair.

"I just thought… I don't know what I thought." She brushed her hand over her perfect cascade of dark brown hair. "I'm your mother. You've always been stronger than me, but I didn't help you as I should've since we've been here, and—"

I stood up then and turned to the stands behind me. Himani was still leaning close to Roan. Fynea was there also putting in a few words. I was sure they were already negotiating something, but I was ready for Himani to get something on camera.

"Himani. You might want to get this." It was important

because this went back to the previous part of the interview. I wanted to be clear.

Himani looked back at one of his camera people who nodded. One of the cameras darted forward, stopping just a few feet from my face.

"Okay," Himani said to me.

"Good."

I turned to my mother and hoped she'd really hear me. "My mother just apologized to me, and it's important that everyone understand that I don't need an apology. Not from anyone. And I won't apologize either. While we were stuck on Earth, we were doing what we had to in order to survive. We did it together for so long, and it's okay that my mother and I did it apart for a little bit. She has nothing to be sorry for or feel guilty about."

I looked down at Lorne. "You didn't do anything wrong either. You had a lot going on here, a lot that you were struggling with, a lot that worked against you going back to Earth, and I completely understand. I'm not mad at you for not coming to get me sooner. If you need my forgiveness, you have it. But you don't need it. Not from me because when I was about to die on that moon, you came for me. You were there the moment that I needed you the most. I was *dying* and you *saved me*. You got there just in time."

I looked at Himani. "You say that the Aunare didn't know or understand what was going on. Okay. That's all in the past. I don't need apologies or explanations from you, the media, the people, or anyone else. I was lucky. I lived. And no matter how much I wish I could change the past and what happened, I can't. No one can. But something can change now. Now you can do something. Now *we* can do something together. Today is a new day. Today we can unite against our enemy."

I paused so that whoever ended up watching this would really, really understand this next part. "Today, we can save everyone who is suffering—Earther and Aunare and halfer—and give them a shot at a better life. It's not going to be easy or quick or painless to get rid of SpaceTech's rule, but billions of lives are on the line. Not just Aunare lives. Everyone. We have the ability to do what's right today. The Aunare are the most powerful people in the universe. If we're united, no one can stand in our way. So, today we unite."

I turned to Eshrin. His skin was darker than most Aunare, and his black hair had a bit of a wave. It wasn't quite as long as Lorne's, but it was enough that he could tie the top part of it back to keep it out of his eyes when we trained.

He was tying it back as he watched me, which meant he wanted to get started. "Are you ready?"

I gave him one short nod. "Ready."

I moved toward him, but my father grabbed my arm, stopping me. He tugged me until I was in his arms.

I froze, unsure of what to do. This wasn't part of my plan. Ever. Why was he doing this? Why was he doing this right now?

Why was he hugging me?

"I knew you'd be a natural at this, but I didn't expect that." He whispered so softly that I wasn't sure I was actually hearing him correctly.

"What?"

"You just gave us all absolution in one breath and hope in the next, even in times as dark as these."

"I did?" I'd just spoken the truth as my heart and soul saw it, and I'd done it for a purpose. To make sure that the Aunare were ready for a fight. But absolution? Hope? That didn't sound like something I would do.

"You did. You are going to be an amazing High Queen. I am truly proud of you, my daughter."

I wasn't sure what to say or what to feel. I pulled away from my father and looked down at Lorne for some help. He rose to stand beside me, and if there was anyone to give hope to people, I knew it had to be him. Not me. It couldn't be me.

I didn't set out to be a leader or to give anyone anything

really. But one look at Lorne's face and I knew he felt the same as my father.

Suddenly it was like everyone was staring at me and expecting so much from me, and it was almost too much to process.

So, instead of figuring out what I was feeling and why, I stepped through the people that loved me and walked to Eshrin. I had a job to do, and today, I'd make that job matter.

"Let's do this," I said quietly to Eshrin.

I glanced over at Roan—who was still sitting next to Himani —and nodded.

He tapped on his wrist unit, turning on my song.

The cameras ensured that today's audience would eventually be much, much larger than the usual, but they weren't physically here. I could forget about them if I focused hard enough. And that's what I was going to do.

I faced the wall.

"Twenty times up fast, and then spar?" Eshrin asked as he stood beside me, shoulder to shoulder.

"Fifteen times up."

"In a hurry to get started?" He grinned down at me. That stony look had already melted as it always did.

I shrugged. "I feel like everything I've been planning for years, everything I've wanted and hoped for but never thought would happen is about to happen." I let out a breath. "I'm here. I'm safe. And I'm about to take SpaceTech down."

The other four guards on duty came to stand beside us. There were a few more on today than normal, but instead of joining in, they kept their eyes on the crowd. They were on duty. But these four were training with me as usual.

Eshrin turned to Camaer, the guard to his right. "Better let Mae'ani know that she's in a mood."

I shoved Eshrin. "I'm not going to hurt you."

He laughed and started counting down in Aunare.

I waited for him to finish counting and then I raced to the wall, with my guards a fraction of a second behind me.

Everything went calm and quiet in my mind as I climbed fast, fast, faster than anyone else could've climbed that wall. And when reached the top flanked on both sides with my guards, I knew I was home.

I was home. I was here. I was safe. And I was in command.

And SpaceTech? They were about to feel the full force of the di Aetes line, backed by all of the Aunare.

And as I flipped to the ground, I felt finally free. My guards landed next to me, and I yelled, "Again!"

We raced back to the wall, faster this time.

This was good. We were a team, and I knew even if it was just us against SpaceTech, I could win.

I would win, and that was everything.

——————

Need more story?
Grab a BONUS extra scene from Lorne's POV

https://inkmonster.net/blog/in-command-bonus-chapter

The story continues with *On Mission,*
Book Four in the Aunare Chronicles series.

Amihanna di Aetes has finally accepted her place in the Aunare world. In a matter of weeks, she'll be their High Queen, but no matter how hard she tries, she finds that she's always doing the wrong thing. At least that's what the High Council keeps telling her...

There's only so much rejection a girl can take, which means she's spending her afternoons trying to get out of High Council meetings. And yet, every time she leaves the council room, she sees the disappointment on her father's face, and worse, on Lorne's face. It pains her, but she can't say what they want her to say.

The council is refusing to see the truth. War isn't just upon the Aunare - they're about to lose.

Training her guards to invade Earth is a much better use of her days. She spent too much time hiding, obeying, forcing herself to do what she had to do to survive.

She's used up all her pretending and can only be who she is. A fighter. A leader. A *warrior*.

ALSO BY AILEEN ERIN

The Complete Alpha Girls Series

Becoming Alpha

Avoiding Alpha

Alpha Divided

Bruja

Alpha Unleashed

Shattered Pack

Being Alpha

Lunar Court

Alpha Erased

The Shadow Ravens Series

Cipher

The Aunare Chronicles

Off Planet

Off Balance

In Command

On Mission

ABOUT THE AUTHOR

Aileen Erin is half-Irish, half-Mexican, and 100% nerd—from Star Wars (prequels don't count) to Star Trek (TNG FTW), she geeks out on Tolkien's linguistics, and has a severe fascination with the supernatural. Aileen has a BS in Radio-TV-Film from the University of Texas at Austin, and an MFA in Writing Popular Fiction from Seton Hill University. She lives with her husband and daughter in Texas, and spends her days doing her favorite things: reading books, creating worlds, and kicking ass.

facebook.com/aelatcham

twitter.com/aileen_erin

instagram.com/aileenerin